DEATH OF A DEAD MAN

DEATH OF A DEAD MAN

A JUNIPER GROVE MYSTERY

KARIN KAUFMAN

CHAPTER 1

The September air was sweet with the perfume of late-blooming roses, and except for the sound of my neighbor, Julia, repeatedly opening and closing her door, all was quiet. Though I'd learned to like Julia in the four months I'd lived in Juniper Grove, she struck me as an easily irritated woman, and something was irritating her on this beautiful morning.

Never mind. The sun was breaking through the pines across the street, warming my face as I stood on my front porch. I was determined to take a walk before the day became too hot and my enthusiasm for exercise flagged.

Now Julia was mumbling. Something about having had it with people. For an instant I considered heading inside and shooting for my back door. There was a lovely walking trail behind my house. But curiosity got the best of me.

"Something wrong, Julia?" I said, standing on tiptoe to peer over the privet hedge between our two houses.

"Rachel, I'm glad you're up." She waved a newspaper with one hand and clutched at her robe with the other. "I need to talk to you."

She disappeared from view, reappearing seconds later on the sidewalk, thumping toward my front door.

"Coffee?" I asked as we headed inside. "You don't look like you've had a chance to make any."

"I know, I know." She glanced down at her robe, scowling. "I realize I'm not dressed, but I need to talk to you before anyone else does."

"That sounds ominous. Have a seat."

She tossed the newspaper onto my kitchen table and sat. "You think you know people. You live in the same place for decades, and you think you know them, but you're wrong."

She was fidgeting now, combing her fingers through her short, pillow-ruffled gray hair. I started the coffee, and while it was brewing I joined her. "Something's really troubling you."

Julia gestured at the paper, touched it, drew back her hand, then took a firm hold of it. "I want you to hear my side of the story, because it's not coming out with that woman in charge."

"What woman?"

"The editor in chief of this rag, Jillian Newsome."

"I don't get the paper," I said, taking it from Julia's hand and setting it on the table before me.

"Very wise."

"What am I looking at?"

"She put it above the fold to make it extra-hard to miss, and there's a sidebar below it on the history of the case." Julia reached over and unfolded the newspaper, pressing it flat.

Immediately the name Foster caught my eye. Julia's last name. "George Foster officially declared dead," I read aloud. Puzzled, I looked to Julia. "But I thought your husband *was* dead. Didn't you say he died years ago?"

"Seven years and five days ago. But they never found his body, so the courts only ruled him dead three days ago. I had to go to court to have them state the obvious."

"I had no idea."

"That's because I don't talk about it, Rachel. Finish reading." She rose and headed for the coffeepot.

"Pour me a cup, will you?" I went back to the paper. George Foster disappeared after stealing $300,000 from his bank, the article reminded everyone. I suppressed an urge to gasp. The bank's vice president and Foster's partner in crime, Mitch Dillard, disappeared at the same time, though Dillard's body was found in the Blue River the next day. Foster's body was never found.

"Here you go. Black?"

"That's fine." I took the cup and tried not to stare gobsmacked at my neighbor. I knew she was a widow—everyone in our town of twelve hundred souls knew that. She had lived in Juniper Grove her entire adult life. "How hard for you."

"Yes, it was," she said simply. "Did you finish reading?"

"Not yet." I took a long sip of coffee, hoping she would fill me in. I didn't even want the *Juniper Grove Post* in my house. I'd sworn off newspapers.

"Well, I'll tell you," she said, dragging the paper her way. "George stole that money, I know that. And then he deserted me. But he died trying to get away. He and Mitch, in the river that same day. He drowned, and the police and the search-and-rescue team that looked for them and found the destroyed raft both testified to that. Body or no body, there was no way George made it out alive."

"But you had to wait seven years."

Julia nodded. "For the official ruling. So I can get his name off this house, off our car, off our bank account. The mess of it all." She massaged her temples.

"You said raft. Why didn't they drive out?"

"They didn't have time. They didn't know it, but they were being watched. The bank didn't normally keep anywhere near that much cash on hand, but George and Mitch waited for the one day they knew money was being transferred."

"And the police knew too?"

"The moment they left the bank. George and Mitch must have been listening to a police scanner, because they took the river to bypass the roadblocks. When they got to the river, they stole the raft from some outfitter. I can't imagine how they thought they'd get away."

I could hardly believe what I was hearing. Roadblocks, a police chase, a river-raft escape. This was Juniper Grove, not Denver. We were sixty miles to the northwest of that city and a whole world away. "Just the two of them on a raft?"

"They knew nothing about rafting on that wild river. How foolish can you get?" She shook her head, disgust in her tone, but I saw tears beginning to well in her eyes.

"But it's over now, Julia. Forget the newspaper. Everyone must know what happened seven years ago, don't you think?"

"Oh yes," Julia said with a rueful laugh. "Jillian Newsome was a reporter back then. She made her career on speculation."

"What did she speculate on?"

"On me." Julia wrapped her fingers around her coffee cup. "She suggested I was involved, that George isn't really dead, and that I got at least part of that $300,000."

Her eyes did not meet mine. She stared into her coffee, waiting for me to speak. My short, sixty-something neighbor involved in a bank heist? At first blush it seemed absurd, and if she had that kind of money, even a third of it, where was it? Her house was in dire need of a fresh coat of paint, her car was an old Ford, and I'd been inside her house—no big-screen TV, no fancy furniture. Julia was a plain woman with plain tastes. Much like me.

"Why are you shaking your head?" Julia asked.

"Well, I mean, it seems so crazy."

"It's a nightmare."

"What's the date on this?" I took hold of the paper and searched the top of the front page. "Day before yesterday."

"The day after the court ruling. You didn't hear anything?"

"I've been in my house, writing." I smiled. "I get so involved sometimes, I forget to get out."

"So now you know."

"I do, but it doesn't matter. And you shouldn't . . ." I fumbled for words. Was she worried I'd look at her with suspicion? I was in Juniper Grove for a fresh start in life, and I wanted to extend that fresh start to her as well. "I'm glad you trusted me with this information, but it doesn't matter, Julia. Never mind that fish wrap of a newspaper. Tomorrow they'll come out with a new edition. People on this street love you. I know, I've seen it."

She tried to smile, her hand rising again to her tousled hair. "Thank you."

"So drink your coffee," I said, motioning with my head at her cup.

Julia did as instructed, but the expression on her face told me the conversation wasn't over.

"We should go get ourselves some scones or cream puffs," I said, forcing a lightheartedness I did not feel into my voice. "I'll treat."

"You and your cream puffs," she said.

"Something else is wrong, isn't it? Spill the beans, come on."

She pulled a folded piece of green paper from her robe pocket and opened it. "I'm far more worried about this, but that awful Newsome woman started it with that article." She slid the paper toward me. "It was taped to my front door this morning."

I unfolded it and read, "You can't fool me. I know what you did seven years ago."

"Who would do that?" she asked. "I've known the people on this street for forty years. I've lived in the same house all that time."

"You should tell the police. Someone was foolish enough to write that in their own hand instead of run it out on a printer. They could trace the handwriting, the ink, the paper."

"Absolutely not." She gulped her coffee, setting her cup back on the table with a little too much force. "I'm not starting *that* again. It would be like poking a rattlesnake."

"Then what are you going to do?"

"I thought maybe . . . I thought, you know . . ."

Realizing what she was asking me, I crossed my arms over my chest, giving her a taste of my don't-even-start body language. "I'm sorry, but no. That's not a good idea. I'm a writer, not—"

"You're a mystery writer, Rachel. You know about

these things."

I leaned forward. "I know the crimes I make up in books. And I lead a very isolated and quiet life."

"And you like it that way, I understand. I'd like my life that way too."

She looked so small and defeated, it broke my heart a little. But how could I help? I dealt with made-up life—life I controlled down to the last comma. Not real life.

When the doorbell rang, I was relieved. Between the kitchen table, the front door, and back again, I would come up with something to say to Julia. She needed to go to the police about the note or forget about it. Or maybe talk to this Jillian Newsome woman and let her know the damage her article had done.

I opened the door to find Holly Kavanagh standing on the top step, holding a small pink box tied with twine. "I'm bearing gifts," she said, extending her hand.

"Is that one of your cream puffs?" The box was obviously from her bakery, Holly's Sweets, so whatever it held was bound to be delicious. I grabbed it and thanked her profusely. "Come in. Want some coffee? Why aren't you at the bakery?"

"My part-timer took over for an hour. I was looking for Julia, and I thought maybe—there you are!" Holly made a beeline for the kitchen table, her long, dark ponytail swinging with each stride.

"Rachel and I are having coffee," Julia said flatly.

Holly took my seat at the table and latched on to Julia's hands. "I need to show you something. I don't want you to worry, but I think you should know about it because it involves more than me, and you know how people talk."

As she retrieved a piece of green paper from her jeans

pocket, Julia gasped.

"Don't tell me," I said, taking a chair. I directed Holly's attention to Julia's note on the table.

"No," Holly breathed. "Like this one?" She unfolded her paper, and there, in the same handwriting as Julia's note, were the words "You can't fool me. I know what you did seven years ago."

"Exactly like that one. What on earth is going on?" I said.

"Seven years," Holly said. "I'm sorry, Julia, but it could only mean one thing." She turned to me. "You weren't here then, Rachel."

"I was working in Boston at the time."

"I've told her all about it," Julia said.

Holly nodded. "Good. Because I have a feeling these notes are going to end up in the *Juniper Grove Post*. You know how I hear the early morning happenings when I open the bakery doors?"

"Otherwise known as gossip?" Julia replied.

"The same note was left on the police department's door, the newspaper's door, the mayor's office, and the town attorney's front door. The front door of his *home*. The attorney is steaming mad. And those are only the places I've heard about. There could be more."

"Who's doing this?" Julia asked. "And what do they want?" She sagged back in her chair and looked from Holly to me.

"It scares me to think someone was at my house in the middle of the night, taping this to my door," Holly said. "I found it when I left for the bakery at 4:00 a.m."

"I've told Julia she should go to the police," I said to Holly. "But you said someone put this same note on the police department's door?"

"That's right. Same wording. Officer Hammond came in—it was his turn to buy donuts—and told me about it. He said the chief was ticked off."

"Then I don't need to say a word to them," Julia declared.

Holly's eyes strayed to Julia's newspaper. "Rachel, if I remember right, you don't get the paper."

"Not on your life." I stood and headed for the coffeemaker, cup in hand. What remained of my coffee had gone cold, and I needed some hot, black caffeine this morning. What was I going to do to help Julia? What *could* I do? "Did you want some coffee, Holly? I'm making a new batch."

"So this paper is Julia's?" she replied.

"It's mine," Julia said.

I turned. The two were exchanging sidelong glances while Holly turned the paper's pages.

"Did you read the article about George?" Holly asked.

"I started to. Why?"

"It continues on page three," she said.

"And?"

"It mentions you," Julia said.

"Why me?"

In answer to my question, Holly read aloud from the paper. "The bank's cash was rumored to be buried somewhere behind 504 Finch Hill Road, on the property now owned by Rachel Stowe, forty-three, formerly of Boston."

I nearly dropped the coffeepot. "Why such detail? Who wrote that?"

"The gracious Ms. Newsome herself."

"But why mention Boston? What's that got to do with anything?" I set the coffeepot back down and retook my seat at the table. "I'm sorry, Julia, I shouldn't complain. Not with what you're going through."

"That's all right," Julia said, patting my hand. "You have a right to be upset."

I was beginning to dislike this editor in chief as much as Julia appeared to. How were the details of my life part of George Foster's story? "And she mentions my age," I said. "That seems gratuitous."

"That's how Newsome rolls," Holly said. "You're not the first bystander to get trolled by her."

Unable to sit still, I rose and strode for the front window, hoping that the sight of my garden would calm me. I was overreacting, feeling testy because my privacy, which I valued, had been invaded for no good reason. But poor Julia. If word of these notes got out—and it would—the *Post* would make her life miserable.

As I surveyed my garden, I saw a Juniper Grove Police Department SUV pull to the curb in front of Julia's house. "Julia, the police are at your house," I said, looking back to her.

"Not a surprise." Her eyes were grim but determined.

"I don't know if I can help you figure out who wrote those notes, but I can try," I said. "How about you, Holly? Let's put our heads together. Meet me here this evening?"

CHAPTER 2

After Julia left my house, finally conceding there was little chance she could avoid the police forever by sitting in my kitchen, my mind raced. So I'd bought a house connected, however obliquely, to a bank robbery. And now, courtesy of the court ruling on George Foster's death, that robbery was in the news again.

I walked to the back of my house, sipping my second cup of coffee. Why would George have buried money here, behind my faux-Victorian house? Had the house been vacant at the time? These were questions I needed to ask Julia tonight. Surely the police had searched the grounds—and inside the house. I slid back the deadbolt on the back door and opened it.

Leaning on the doorjamb, I looked at the foothills—so near I could almost touch them—once again thanking God for bringing me home. I was a Colorado girl by birth, but I'd lived more than seven years in Boston, working as senior editor at a publishing house. By the end of those years I'd turned short-tempered and stern. The endless meetings, the sniping about corner offices and how many coffees we could rightfully drink, the prim city wardrobes—I'd had my fill.

Not to say that I moved to this little town nestled against the foothills because here I could wear jeans every day, though the idea appealed to me every Boston morning as I slipped into dresses and heels. I'm a hiking boots kind of girl.

For more than seven years I scrimped and saved, calculating that I could live in a small town like Juniper Grove on very little money. Which is good, because very little was what I had. I began to write mysteries before I left Boston, and I found a company willing to publish them. My mysteries weren't big sellers, but maybe one day. In the meantime, with no children or husband to spend money on, my savings and a small inheritance from my parents were more than enough.

I heard my doorbell and imagined Julia back again, needing to commiserate, but when I opened the door, I was greeted instead by two police officers. Smiling ones, thankfully.

"Ma'am, I'm Police Chief James Gilroy and this is Officer Hammond. Have you got a moment?"

"This is about the notes people found on their doors this morning?"

Chief Gilroy raised an eyebrow. "Did you get one too?"

"No, I didn't. Come in." I stepped back from the doorway and motioned them inside. "Can I get you coffee?"

"No, thank you," Gilroy answered quickly, before Officer Hammond, who looked as though he wanted nothing more than caffeine at that moment, could answer.

I pointed at my kitchen table. "Have a seat."

"We'll only be here a minute," Gilroy said, remaining standing.

Officer Hammond wanted to sit, I could tell. He

wanted to sit and have a cup of coffee and a donut. He didn't look particularly energetic, despite the fact that he appeared to be five to ten years younger than Gilroy. But Hammond had one of those approachable faces. Friendly and open.

Gilroy, on the other hand, was all business. Dark hair and ice blue eyes. Not friendly. I'd sized him up in all of sixty seconds, which perhaps wasn't fair. On the plus side, he wasn't wearing a police uniform or even a tie with his suit jacket.

"You talked to Julia, my neighbor?" I asked.

"We did. We're canvassing the neighborhood, asking if anyone saw or heard anything unusual last night."

"I didn't. I understand the police department got one of those notes too."

"Yep," Hammond said.

"Do you live here alone?" Gilroy asked.

"Yes. Why? Do you think this note writer is dangerous?"

"I doubt it, but keep your doors locked. It's good policy at any time."

"Someone familiar with the goings-on seven years ago must have written those notes."

Gilroy said nothing. He dug around his inside jacket pocket and then presented me with his business card. "Call me if you see or hear anything."

I took his card. "Are you really going to try to find out who wrote the notes?"

Gilroy looked at me as though I'd asked the strangest question he'd heard in years. "That's why I'm here."

"It's just that in Boston, since the notes don't threaten anyone, they wouldn't even—"

"This isn't Boston."

"Well, I'm not *from* Boston." I was about to recite my Colorado bona fides but decided against it. It was none of his business, and anyway, he was moving for the door and I had questions to ask. "I understand that some people think George Foster buried cash on my property."

Officer Hammond, who had been following Gilroy to the door, turned back, a grin on his face. "For a year after the theft we had treasure hunters digging holes in your backyard. That's why the previous owners put up a fence."

"Is that why I'm supposed to be careful?" Hammond was the one talking, but I addressed my question to Gilroy.

"There's nothing buried in your yard," Gilroy said. "Foster and Dillard took off right after leaving the bank. They didn't stop to dig holes."

"Are you looking for a stranger or a local on this note thing?" I asked.

"We're not looking for anyone in particular right now," Gilroy answered. "Just gathering information."

"Were you two living in town when all this happened?"

"I'd just become police chief," Gilroy said.

"And I was an officer," Hammond said. "Just like I am now."

Gilroy threw Hammond a quick look—too quick for me to read with accuracy, but it wasn't an expression of approval.

"How many people reported getting notes?" I asked.

"Give me a call if you see or hear anything."

Most people display awkward mannerisms when avoiding questions they don't want to answer. A twitch of the lips, a telltale nose scratch. Not Gilroy. He kept on trucking. My question wasn't even a speed bump in his road.

I shut the door behind them and watched them jog down my steps and hop into their SUV, its side emblazoned with the words "Juniper Grove Police Department" in blue letters. In a town this size, were Gilroy and Hammond the only police? I didn't know. But I surmised that Gilroy and Hammond hardly ever dealt with crime, and I wondered if George Foster had survived his raft trip and escaped because of their inexperience.

Foster's body had never been found. Wasn't that uncommon? If he had taken that raft trip with Mitch Dillard, and Dillard's body had been found, why hadn't Foster's? More important, had Julia considered the possibility that her husband was still alive?

Another thought occurred to me as I undid the twine from Holly's bakery box: Julia might have been covering for her husband all these years. I shook my head, dismissing the notion. Julia didn't have a sneaky bone in her body, let alone the guile to help fake her husband's death and shield his ill-gotten money.

I took a large bite of the cream puff, its filling oozing out the sides as I dug in. Holly was a wizard, and her puff pastry was the best I had ever tasted, hands down. I knew what her cream puffs were doing to my waistline—how much had I gained since moving to town?—and frankly, I didn't care.

Not true. I cared a little. I'd started gaining weight in Boston and I'd doubled down in Juniper Grove. Before I knew it, I'd put on twenty pounds, maybe more. Tomorrow I'd hike the trail behind my house, no excuses. I put the cream puff in the refrigerator as a treat after what I was sure would be a troublesome investigation in town. If I was going to help Julia, I'd need to poke around, and I had a feeling I was going to put a few noses out of joint.

I grabbed my car keys from a hook by the back door and headed down the narrow brick path that led to my garage, a detached shed of sorts behind my house.

"First question," I said out loud as I drove down Finch Hill Road on my way downtown, "who got the notes? Second question, what connection did any of them, or all of them, have to the bank theft and disappearance of George Foster?"

I was heading for Holly's Sweets on Main Street, a three-minute drive from my house. Holly had found one of the notes on her door, and she was likely to possess more unbiased information about the events of seven years ago than Julia. Besides, her bakery, which opened before any other shop downtown, was a repository of town gossip. People stopped by for a muffin or scone on their way to work and opened up to her. Fortunately for those people, Holly herself was not a spreader of gossip. But she was Julia's friend, and if she had heard something that might help us find the note writer, she would tell me.

The morning rush had ended, and only one customer remained in the bakery, a fifty-something woman with auburn hair cut in a bob. The first thing I noticed about a person, man or woman, was the hair. I don't know why, except maybe my own hair—dark with streaks of gray, limp, shoulder length, and plain—was a continual source of frustration to me.

When Holly saw me, she smiled and greeted me as just another customer, inviting me to examine the fresh cakes under glass domes on her countertop as though I'd called earlier and ordered one. She didn't need to ask twice. Swaths of frosting—pink, white, chocolate, and buttercream, probably. I was so enchanted by the cakes I didn't notice the woman with the bobbed hair was leaving until I heard the bakery door's bell ring.

Holly leaned forward, her arms on the counter, and began to talk excitedly. "Well that's timing for you. Can you believe she was in here?"

"Who is she?"

"Oh, of course." She waved her hands, shooing away her foolish question. "I keep forgetting you're new here. It seems like I've known you for years."

I grinned. What a nice thing for her to say.

"Anyway," Holly went on, "that was Belinda Almond. To cut to the chase, she was having an affair with George Foster in the months before he died."

"No." I was stunned. And I felt protective of Julia, though I knew nothing about her marriage. How dare he do that to her? If George had been there, I'd have given him what for. "Did Julia know?"

"She did." Holly came around the counter, marched for the shop window, and glanced up and down the sidewalk before spinning back to me. She had news, and she needed to tell me before another customer arrived.

"Was Belinda Almond connected to the bank theft?" I asked.

Holly lifted her shoulders. "That's what a lot of people want to know. What I do know is Belinda got one of those notes this morning."

"You're joking."

"She was royally upset, kept talking about being dragged back in to the whole thing and how she thought she was finally free of it."

"That's how Julia feels."

"I almost said that to her."

"You didn't tell her about Julia's note?"

"Never. Belinda's a customer, and I treat her with civility, but I don't like her. I'm sorry to say that, but what she did to Julia was terrible."

"Who else knows about Belinda's affair with George?"

Holly gave a small shake of her head. "In this little town? Everyone. Especially after seven years."

"Doesn't Belinda feel uncomfortable with everyone knowing that?"

"You would think."

"That's probably why she's upset—I mean, aside from getting the note."

"Because people will start talking again."

And keep on talking, I thought. Because this note writer wasn't going to stop. Whoever it was, he hadn't placed all those notes on all those doors just to drop it now and go away. He had a plan and was just getting started.

"That's not all," Holly said. "A young man, maybe in his early twenties, was in here half an hour ago. I've never seen him before, and I know everyone in town. He asked me what happened to our former mayor, and I said he died two years ago. He seemed disappointed. Not sad, but like he missed an opportunity. I started to tell him we have a new mayor, Douglas McDermott, but he interrupted and asked me about Chief Gilroy. He asked if I thought he was a good cop."

"And you said . . . ?"

"I said yes, he's good, and our almost nonexistent

crime rate is proof of it." Holly paused for effect. "He laughed at me. Brayed like a donkey. It gave me the creeps, Rachel."

I walked to one of the small tables on the bakery's far wall and sat. "Chief Gilroy and Officer Hammond were on the force when George Foster and Mitch Dillard stole that money." I was stating what Holly already knew, but I needed to get the facts straight in my mind. "And a note was taped to the police department's door?" I looked to Holly for confirmation.

"That's right," she said, taking the chair across from mine.

"And the mayor got a note, but on his office door, not on his home."

"Right. McDermott himself told me that. He was my first customer, early this morning. He saw the note on his way here, taped to the door of his office building."

"And the town attorney?"

"Tom Ventura. He was in this morning too, only he woke up to one of those notes on the front door of his house, like I did."

"He told you?"

"By then I'd heard about McDermott and the police department, so I asked him if he'd heard about this note people were finding around town. His eyes popped, but he looked relieved to talk about it."

"What was Tom Ventura doing seven years ago?"

"He was town attorney back then too."

"So the only new face is McDermott."

"He was around back then, but he wasn't mayor. What are you thinking?"

"I need to write all this down." It was how I solved

problems—in real life or in novels. I had to write things down, organize, see the facts before me on paper.

"So many new names for you to remember. Do you think we'll solve this mystery?"

I answered with conviction. "Yes, I think so." But with growing anxiety, I sensed that the annoying notes would soon be the least of our worries. "Would you ask around, see if you can find out who that young man is?"

CHAPTER 3

Julia was staring at the pen I'd given her, turning it over in her hands. "You're both wonderful for helping me, but I don't think I can add anything. I woke up, went outside to sit on the porch, and found the note on my door, that's all."

"If we're going to solve this," I said, handing her a notepad, "we need to talk about more than what you found taped to your door. This didn't start with anonymous notes." I gave Holly a pen and notepad too and then took a seat at my kitchen table.

"I suppose not," Julia reluctantly agreed. "It started seven years ago."

"Though I have a suspicion we've already found the note writer," I added.

Holly straightened. "That strange man in my bakery, by any chance?"

"What strange man?" Julia asked.

"Did you find out who he was?" I asked.

"He's staying at the Lilac Lane Bed and Breakfast—under the name Joe Smith." Holly folded her arms and shot me a knowing look. "Joe Smith. Sure."

"I figured as much," I said, making note of the name on my legal pad. "How did you find out?"

"A friend who owns Grove Coffee talked to him, loosened his tongue with caffeine."

Julia huffed. “Is someone going to tell me?”

I quickly explained how Holly had met this Joe Smith, a stranger in town, adding, “He thought the old mayor was still alive and still the mayor. Holly said he seemed disappointed to learn he wasn’t. I think he was disappointed to find out his note on the mayor’s office targeted the wrong man.”

“But the other notes hit the right targets,” Holly said.

“I think so.”

“Why would a stranger do this?” Julia said.

“He may be a stranger to Juniper Grove,” I said, “but somehow he’s connected to what happened seven years ago. We’ll find out.”

“It’s going to be the talk of the town,” Julia said. “How many people or places got these wretched notes?”

“Six,” Holly said.

Julia counted off on her fingers. Looking bewildered, she counted again. “How so?”

Holly lowered her voice, as if whispering would soften the blow. “Belinda Almond got one.”

Julia’s eyes squeezed shut. “Not her too.”

It was then I realized how tired my normally energetic neighbor looked. And I began to see that this battle with the past was probably why she had seemed so irritable since I’d first moved in next door. She had to have been dealing with the courts for months prior to the final ruling, and now some coward was holding her up to town ridicule. Judging by Holly’s description, Joe Smith was not a kind man, and if I was right about him being the note writer, Julia was in for more trouble.

“You’re very brave for letting us dredge this up again,” I said. “It can’t be easy.”

"I asked you to do it, and I'm going to see it through," she said, her chin rising in defiance. "Let people think what they want. And if they have opinions, they had better keep them to themselves."

Most of the time Julia had a grandmotherly air about her, and I liked that, but every now and then she transformed into someone you did not want to mess with. I liked that too. "First we need to find out who Joe Smith really is," I said.

"How do we do that?" Holly asked.

"Do you know who runs the B&B?"

"Only that it's a woman, but I don't remember her name, and I don't know anyone who works there, either. I can ask around town."

"Not yet," I said. "Let's keep this quiet. Tomorrow I'll check out their parking lot and look for out-of-state plates. Maybe Joe Smith doesn't live in Colorado."

Holly bristled with enthusiasm. "I can help with that."

"I should do this alone," I said. "He doesn't know me, but obviously he knows you. We don't want to tip him off. I'll also try to get a look at the Lilac Lane's register, if it's not computerized."

"Do you need me to go with you to distract the receptionist?" Julia said.

I grinned. Despite my belief that this whole affair was about to get dangerous, I was having fun. And the conversation was beginning to work wonders on Julia, who was now sitting straight as a rod, her eyes alight. "Let me see what I can do first," I said. "If I need help, I'll call you in for backup."

Holly was writing down names on her legal pad, a frown forming on her face. "Six people or places," she said.

"The police, the mayor, Belinda Almond, Tom Ventura, Julia . . ." She looked up. "Something's been bothering me. Why did I get a note? I was here at the time, living in the same house, married to Peter, but I wasn't involved. Everyone else was directly involved—or they were like Tom Ventura, holding public office."

"Was Peter connected in any way?" I said.

"No, and Caleb was only six at the time."

"Then that's something else we need to find out. But it could be as simple as you and Julia are close friends."

"You supported me when a lot of other people didn't," Julia said.

"Maybe the note writer considers that your crime," I said. For the first time since the whole note thing started, Holly looked worried, and immediately I wanted to pull those words back. "What I mean is, he seems to be casting a wide net, targeting people only vaguely connected. I bet tomorrow we'll find out that even more people found notes."

Julia rapped the table with her knuckles. "The police will ride that Joe Smith out on a rail."

"I don't know about that," I said. Leaning back in my seat, I went over the conversation I'd had with Chief Gilroy in my head. He seemed to take the notes seriously. Either that or he was miffed by the nuisance they presented. But was he really going to track down the note writer? And if he found him, what would he charge him with?

"Chief James Gilroy does not play around with crime," Julia said. "He's the best thing that ever happened to Juniper Grove."

"You just like his blue eyes," Holly said with a grin.

"Stop that," Julia said.

I shook my head. "But what crime has the note writer committed?"

"There's got to be a statute," Holly said.

"Maybe there is, but I'll bet the most the police can do is cite him for some minor infraction and make him pay a fine."

"Like a parking ticket?"

Julia looked crestfallen. "But that won't solve anything. He'll just keep writing."

"If he does, then the police can do more," I said. "You can't keep breaking the same law, no matter how small."

"I hope so," Julia said. "And even if the police can't stop him, I need to know why he's doing this."

"We need to find out who Joe Smith is," Holly said, "and I mean right away."

I rose and began to slowly pace the kitchen floor. A kitchen table discussion could take us only so far. We needed more information, and we needed to act. "We can't assume Smith is the note writer. What we can assume is that he's not on good terms with Chief Gilroy."

"Which makes him a very suspicious character," Julia said.

"We can also wonder why a stranger would want to question Holly about the mayor and the police chief," I continued.

"We're certain he's a stranger?" Holly asked.

"He didn't know who our current mayor is. He's a stranger or a new arrival."

"I see." Holly sprang from her seat. "I've got an idea. Let's head over to the B&B, right now. Julia and I can stay in the car while you check the parking lot. I get up at four o'clock in the morning, so in less than an hour I'll be dead to the world."

"That's not a bad idea," I said. "For all we know, he and his car will be gone by tomorrow morning."

"You're both serious?" Julia said. "This time of night?"

"You don't have to go, Julia," I said.

"Oh no," she said, pushing herself from her chair, "you're not leaving me to sit at home and watch TV. If you two are going, so am I."

I grabbed my pale teal jacket—thrilled that with the chilly September nights I could start wearing it again—and headed for the back door and garage, Holly and Julia following.

Holly got in first, sliding into the back of my Subaru Forester, and Julia took the front seat. "Do you need to tell Peter?" I asked Holly, backing away from the garage.

"No, it's fine," she said. "I've got my cell, and he knows I'm with you two."

My house was about as far from the B&B as it was from Holly's Sweets, just a three- or four-minute drive. The heart of Main Street—I loved that it was actually called Main Street—was only four blocks long. In fact, downtown itself was only four blocks east to west and three blocks north to south. But it was a lively place. A place where people walked, leaving their cars behind. Where neighbors greeted each other, stopped to chat, stopped to literally smell the flowers in dozens of planters, pots, and hanging baskets.

I pulled to the curb outside the B&B, a block north of the bakery on Lilac Lane. The owner, having taken the street name seriously, had painted the place a vibrant lilac color, though the shock of that color was somewhat dampened by its white trim.

I took a flashlight from my glove box and told Julia and Holly to stay in the car while I checked out the parking lot. As I started for the B&B, it occurred to me that a woman checking license plates with a flashlight might raise the eyebrows of any guest who happened to be looking out a window, so I pocketed the flashlight, hoping lights in the lot would be sufficient. Then again, a woman walking up and down a parking lot without getting into a car was suspicious all on its own.

There was no crime in looking at license plates, but I didn't want to alert Joe Smith, or whoever he was, to my actions. If he knew someone was onto him, he would disappear from view. Though I was sure he wasn't going to leave town altogether until he'd fulfilled his real purpose.

It didn't take long to scan the plates in the well-lit lot. There were only a dozen cars, most of them from Colorado, but also two from Wyoming, one from Idaho, and one from Utah. As discreetly as possible, I took photos of the out-of-state plates with my phone, the flash turned off.

"Four out-of-state plates," I said, returning to my Forester.

Holly grabbed my arm. "Look, you two."

I followed her gaze out the window.

"Jillian Newsome just came out of the B&B," Holly said. "And Joe Smith is right behind her."

"Oh, wouldn't you just know it," Julia said, glaring at the pair of them. "The man we're searching for is with Jillian Newsome? Just wouldn't you know it. Oh, I'm . . . I'm . . ." Her hackles were going up, I could tell.

"Shh," Holly said. "Get down or they'll see us."

Julia dutifully slid down in her seat until only her head was above the window frame.

"It doesn't matter if she sees me," I said, looking back to Holly, who had thrown herself sideways on the back seat. "So that's the legendary editor in chief of the *Juniper Grove Post*." In her mid-forties, tall and thin with long brown hair and rather soft and doughy features, Jillian Newsome didn't look like the sort of woman to inspire either fear or anger. She looked professional but harmless.

"She's in cahoots with Joe Smith," Holly whispered.

"Of course she is," Julia said.

"The *Post* comes out every other day?" I asked.

"That's right," Julia said. "Thank goodness it's no more often than that. That woman has ambitions, and she'll move on to a daily paper. Hopefully very soon."

"So the next paper comes out tomorrow morning. Can you bring me your copy, Julia?"

For a moment Julia was silent. "You want to see what information Joe Smith is giving her?"

"Or what the two are concocting together," I said.

"Maybe she hired him," Holly said, still talking under her breath. "To get the story going again."

"They're leaving," I said. "Smith into the B&B, and Newsome is walking to the parking lot."

Grunting, Julia straightened in her seat, and as Newsome drove her SUV onto the street, she and Holly turned their faces from the windows.

"You know," Holly said, "this itself could be a big story. Newspaper editor conspires with out-of-towner to terrorize the residents of Juniper Grove."

"We need to find out more," I said.

"We found out a lot tonight," Holly said.

Smiling, I looked back to Holly. "We sure did. This was a great idea." There we were, three friends on a stakeout. A single writer in her forties, a married bakery owner in her thirties, and a widow in her sixties. Was there a more unlikely crew?

"But I'm afraid I'm fading fast," Holly said apologetically.

I started the engine and pulled from the curb. Holly needed her sleep. Bakery owners had to rise at ridiculous hours. We were silent as we drove back to my house. I was considering the various reasons for Jillian Newsome to meet with Joe Smith, none of them innocent, and Julia and Holly were drifting off. What tack I took next would depend on what news the *Juniper Grove Post* brought tomorrow. I had a feeling the front page was going to be devoted to the Great Juniper Grove Notes Scandal. Poor Julia.

"We're here," I said, pulling into the garage. "Anyone forget anything in my house?"

"Nope," Holly said, exiting the Forester.

"I should have dropped you off at your house," I said.

"No problem. I'll go through your kitchen and out your front door."

Julia stirred herself and climbed out of the SUV. "I'll see you tomorrow with the newspaper," she said.

"Early," I said. We headed into my backyard, walking up the brick path.

"That wasn't there before," Holly said, pointing at a shovel on the path.

"No, it wasn't." I halted. "What's that to the side?"

"You need lights back here," Holly said, circling

around me.

Instantly I knew what I was looking at. “No, stop.” I yanked on her arm.

“What?”

Julia gasped. “Is that . . . ?”

“A body,” I said. “There’s a body in my backyard.”

Holly backed up. “Who is it?”

“I can’t tell.” I edged forward, Julia and Holly close behind me. “I think it’s a man, but he’s on his side. Only part of his face is showing.” Pulling out the flashlight I’d stuck in my jacket pocket, I switched it on and trained the light on his face.

Julia gasped again, louder this time. I wheeled back.

“It can’t be,” she said, her hands clutching at her breastbone. “It’s impossible. That’s George. That’s my husband.”

CHAPTER 4

When I'd first spotted George Foster's body, I hadn't seen the hole in the ground next to him, but now Chief Gilroy was shining a light on it—a large hole between Foster and my daffodil bed. "Sorry to make you come out here and look at this," he said.

"I already saw the body." *Though not with giant floodlights illuminating it*, I thought. I could tell now Foster had been hit with the shovel that was still on the brick path. There was a dark, wet patch that looked like blood on the back of his head and a smaller wet patch on the shovel blade.

"You're sure you or your yard people didn't dig it?"

"I'm positive, and I don't have yard people." As if I'd dig an enormous hole and forget about it.

"I had to check. It's September—I thought you might have been planting a tree."

"Oh."

"And that's not your shovel?" he asked.

"No, I have two shovels in the garage, and neither of them looks like that."

"Thanks. You can go back inside."

I backed well away from the hole but remained in my yard, watching Officer Hammond string crime tape in a wide rectangle around the body, using trees and shrubs as anchors. I'd written about crime scenes in my books, but I'd never actually seen one. Another officer, younger than Gilroy by a couple decades, was examining the ground around the body, running his flashlight in arcs over the grass. Then there *were* more than two people in the Juniper Grove police force. There were at least three.

"Chief Gilroy," I said, "does Juniper Grove have a forensics unit?"

"Ma'am, you need to go back inside, please," he said. "I'll be there in a minute. I have to talk to you and your friends before they go home."

I reluctantly joined Holly and Julia at the kitchen table. Holly was doing a masterful job of staying awake, all things considered. Seeing the notepads I'd handed out earlier spread over the table, I rushed to scoop them up before Gilroy could see them.

"Did you call your husband?" I asked Holly.

"I told him I'd be late, that's all. I'll explain things when I get home."

I sat down next to Julia and put an arm around her shoulders. "I'm so sorry."

"I'm all right, Rachel."

In the shock of the moment, finding her dead husband truly dead after all these years, she had cried. But briefly, and more with regret than anguish, I thought. After that, a sort of frozen calm had come over her.

"He really wasn't dead," Holly said.

"He may as well have been," Julia replied.

Gilroy popped his head around the back door, then entered the kitchen hesitantly, his eyes on Julia. "Mrs. Foster, I'd like to have a word, if you're up to it."

"I'm quite up to it," Julia said. "I've had seven years

to get over George's death. But I think you should talk to Holly Kavanagh first. She gets up early in the morning to open the bakery downtown."

Holly lifted her chin from her hand and flashed a weak smile.

"I understand you live across the street," Gilroy said, looking to Holly.

"Across and two houses down."

"Can you think of anything to add to what you and your friends told me when I first got here?"

Holly thought a moment. "Not really. We're certain he wasn't there when we got into the car. That's about it."

"That's enough for now, then. You'll be at the bakery tomorrow?"

"All morning, but please don't come in before eight-thirty. It's crazy before then."

Holly gave Julia a hug, whispered something in her ear, and headed out the front door. I doubted if she'd get much sleep tonight.

With Holly gone, Gilroy turned his attentions to me, asking me to tell him once again when the three of us had left the house and returned. Was he hoping I'd slip up? Reveal that we had never left and had in fact stayed at home to murder the once-dead George Foster? "I don't see why I have to keep going over the same things," I complained. "It's like Holly said, there's not much to tell."

"I understand," Gilroy said, "but sometimes going over the same ground shakes up details you didn't remember on first telling."

"Trouble is, there aren't any details. We went out, we came back, and there was George Foster."

"Where did you go?"

I'd taken the trouble to hide the notepads from Gilroy, but now he was asking me a direct question. Lying was out of the question. You don't lie to police officers—I'd been taught that as a child—and I couldn't involve Julia in deception, which is what I'd be doing if I lied to Gilroy with her sitting silently next to me. "You know those anonymous notes?"

Gilroy said nothing.

"Well, we think we know who wrote them. He came into Holly's bakery this morning and—"

"Holly Kavanagh?" he asked. "Who was just here?"

"Yes, *that* Holly Kavanagh who owns a bakery."

"Go on."

"He's registered as Joe Smith at the Lilac Lane B&B. He asked Holly some very odd questions, and he was meeting with Jillian Newsome—that's the editor in chief of the *Juniper Grove Post*—at the B&B tonight. We think they're working together to resurrect the Foster and Dillard story. So to speak."

"That's a lot of detail."

"You didn't ask until now about what we were doing. You asked about the body."

"I should have broadened my question."

There was that stern look again. Steely eyes, tight mouth. Looking at him, I couldn't help but notice how handsome he was, despite his obvious disapproval of me. He had what people like to call chiseled features—a strong nose, good cheekbones. His hair was still dark for the most part, but there were slivers of gray at the temples and hairline.

"Would you like some coffee?" I asked.

He seemed taken aback by the sudden shift. "Sure.

Thanks. Some for Officers Hammond and Underhill too?"

"You bet." I stood and glanced down at Julia, who was sitting hunched at the table, needing very much, I suspected, to be alone with her thoughts. "Can Julia go home now? I can answer any other questions you have."

"Another few minutes. I'm sorry, Mrs. Foster, bear with us. You can go home soon."

"I'm all right," she said for the third or fourth time since finding George.

No, she wasn't.

As I started the coffee, glad to have something to do with my hands, Gilroy began to question Julia. He said he needed to ask her once more, though she'd no doubt heard the question many times before, if George had contacted her since disappearing seven years ago. Things had changed, he said, and he wouldn't be doing his job if he didn't ask her. It seemed he was being as gentle as possible, given the circumstances.

"He never contacted me," Julia said, her voice firm. "Ever. I was sure he was dead—and so were you and Officer Hammond, if you'll recall. Both of you testified to that in court."

"Yes, we did."

"You found the broken raft and Mitch Dillard's body."

"I remember."

"But somehow George survived, didn't he?"

"Yes, somehow."

"And in all this time he never told me he was still alive."

"I'm sorry."

I turned and leaned against the kitchen counter,

watching Julia.

"Even if I still loved him, I'm not sure I could forgive him for what he's put me through," she said. "He stole money, he deserted me, and he hurt a lot of people, so I'm not very fond of him. I'd tell you if he'd contacted me recently."

Officer Hammond strode in through the back door, his eyes going first to Gilroy and then to the coffee cups I'd lined on the counter.

"Coffee, Officer?" I asked.

"Can I? Thank you."

Hierarchical etiquette probably demanded that I serve Gilroy first, but Hammond looked in desperate need of caffeine. I poured him a cup, handed it to him, and pointed at the refrigerator. "There's half and half in the fridge."

Next I poured Gilroy a cup, then myself, and I told Hammond to let Underhill know there was coffee to be had inside.

"Chief," Hammond said, "the forensics team from county is here."

"I'll start another pot," I said.

Drinking his coffee, Hammond eyed Julia over the rim of his cup. The goodwill Julia had garnered over the years as a widow, and the sympathy she'd gained through the court's declaration that George Foster was indeed dead, was evaporating. Julia was in for a world of trouble that would probably eclipse the pain of the previous seven years. I knew she hadn't killed George—that was obvious—but I also believed down to my soul that she'd never been involved in George's crime and that all along she had thought George was dead. But how could I help her by proving that?

I took my cup to the table and sat next to Julia. "Does that hole have something to do with the money that's supposedly buried in my backyard?" I asked Gilroy.

"I doubt it."

A man of few words.

"If George was looking for it," I added, "then he really did bury it back there. Somehow he was able to before he and Mitch Dillard ran."

"Not necessarily," Gilroy replied. "Let's not jump to conclusions."

"The previous owners of this house, Mrs. Foster," Hammond said, edging toward the table, "did they ever try looking for money?"

"Not that I know of, but it's not like I watched them all the time."

"Your husband never came back from the bank that day, even for five minutes?" Hammond asked.

"I've said no a thousand times. He left for work and I never saw him again. You can search my yard and house for the fifth time if you like," Julia said. "Or my bank account. The police and courts have poked into that any number of times, but be my guest."

"I'm sorry, ma'am," Hammond said, holding up a hand in self-defense, "but you have to admit it's strange he'd show up dead three days after being declared dead."

"You don't have to tell *me* it's strange," Julia said, raking her fingers through her hair.

"What reason would he have for never contacting you?" Hammond asked.

"You can go home now, Mrs. Foster," Gilroy said before Julia could answer. "We can finish this tomorrow."

Hammond cocked an eyebrow and shot Gilroy a

questioning look, but in deference to his chief, he said nothing.

The sound of voices on my front step made me turn. "Are your officers in my front yard?" I asked, pointing toward the door.

"They're all in back," Gilroy said. "Neighbors?"

"Not chattering away like that."

A camera flash hit me as soon as I opened the door. When my eyes cleared, I saw Jillian Newsome and a photographer on my front step. "What on earth?"

"Rachel Stowe?" Newsome said.

"It's after ten at night," I said, rather feebly.

"I didn't think you'd be sleeping," she said with a grin. She pivoted slightly and spread her arms out, bidding me to notice the police cars and forensics van parked in front of my house.

"Sleep has nothing to do with it. You don't knock on a stranger's door at night then pop a flash in her face." I moved to close the door, but Jillian blocked me, sticking out her arm and throwing a foot over the threshold.

"Can we talk? My photographer can stay out here, and I promise no more photos of you, just your house."

"You're taking photos of my house?"

I heard the rustling of an angry Julia behind me, fast approaching.

"Jillian Newsome?" I said. "Have I got the name right? I'm assuming the *Juniper Grove Post* has an owner."

"If you're trying to intimidate me, I'm only doing my job," Newsome said.

Julia came up beside me and jerked the door wide, smoldering with anger. In an instant the photographer raised his camera and clicked it several times, rapid fire.

"You people!" Julia said.

A chair scraped on the kitchen floor behind me, and in another second, Gilroy too was at the door. "You're on private property, ma'am, and I believe the homeowner asked you to leave."

"She didn't ask anything of the kind," Newsome said.

"I'm asking you now," I said.

Officer Hammond joined us at the door, alongside Gilroy.

When the photographer raised his camera, Gilroy took a step forward. "I don't think you should do that again."

A simple, essentially nonthreatening statement, but coming from the granite-faced Gilroy, it carried great force. The photographer lowered his camera and took a backward step.

Not to be dissuaded so easily, Newsome fixed her eyes on the chief. "Chief Gilroy, you were on the case seven years ago. Why is it you never found George Foster? Until tonight, that is."

"Come by the station tomorrow and I'll be glad to answer your questions," Gilroy said as he started to shut the door.

Newsome pulled back her foot. "Is this sort of shoddy police work why you were forced to leave Fort Collins for little Juniper Grove?" she shouted as the door closed in her face.

Behind us, someone cleared his throat, and in unison the four of us turned. Another officer, it had to be Underhill, was standing in the kitchen, his hands and his forearms covered in dirt. "We found something in the bottom of the hole, just under a layer of dirt," he said. "It was in a cardboard box. Kinda weird. We thought it was a dead pet at first. Like a turtle or a fish. You know how kids bury their pets."

"What is it, Underhill?" Gilroy asked impatiently.

"It's a piece of paper signed by George Foster. It's kind of hard to read, but it looks like it says, 'Chief Gilroy is a liar.'"

CHAPTER 5

Despite my lack of sleep, I was up early the next morning, hoping Julia would show up soon with the *Juniper Grove Post*. Or without it. I needed to see her, to make sure she was okay. I didn't care how many times she insisted she was all right. My friend was heartbroken. Her world had been shattered once again.

It wasn't just discovering her long-lost husband's body. She was also upset—perhaps equally upset—by the piece of paper Officer Underhill had found in my backyard. After all, George Foster had been dead to Julia for seven years, but Chief Gilroy was very much alive and, in her mind, very much admired. Before leaving my house last night, she'd asked me, "Why would George write that about the chief?"

I pondered the question myself as I fixed coffee and buttered toast. Julia had confirmed the handwriting on the paper was George's, ruling out a prank by one of the treasure hunters. George had thought it was important to declare in writing that Chief Gilroy was a liar. So why bury that declaration? It made no sense.

It made even less sense that the paper Officer Underhill found had been torn from the bottom of a larger sheet. George had written more, but he had chosen to tear that particular strip from his page and bury it.

But why try to dig it up after seven years? Maybe something else had been buried in that hole along with the box—something the killer took. One thing seemed certain. Either someone had gone with him to my backyard or someone had followed him there and taken George by surprise. Death had finally caught up with George Foster.

Cracking open my front door, I scanned the curb for Jillian Newsome and her flash-happy photographer. Not seeing them, I stepped outside, looking and listening for Julia. She was probably still asleep, I reasoned. Best not to disturb her after last night.

But I was ready to act. First I needed the morning paper, then I needed to talk to Holly. Chances were she hadn't heard about the piece of paper Underhill had found. Gilroy was probably keeping mum on that. I also needed to find out how the other note recipients, Tom Ventura and Douglas McDermott, were involved in the Foster-Dillard case. Though McDermott's note was probably a misstep, taped to the mayor's office door by an unknowing Joe Smith, who hadn't realized the old mayor had left office.

I hastily ate my toast, gulped my coffee, and slipped a few quarters into my jeans pocket. Then I darted out the back door, slowing as I neared the hole. I ducked under the crime tape, still strung between trees, and stopped. Holly had rightly pointed out that I needed lights in the backyard. There weren't any on the garage, and the low-watt light by my back door was off most of the time. I had come to Juniper Grove to get away from all the bright lights—and the reasons for them. Truth was, George could have been digging in my backyard before Julia, Holly, and I got into my car. If he had hidden behind shrubs as I walked to my garage, I wouldn't have seen him.

I eased the Forester out of the garage and made two quick lefts before I was back on Finch Hill Road, driving for downtown. Here and there were gentle reminders that autumn was on the way. A sumac tinged with red, cottonwood trees wearing small patches of yellow, like badges, in their upper branches. What a beautiful time of year.

Minutes later I was a block from Holly's Sweets, which I soon realized was as close as I would get to the busy bakery at that hour of the morning. I parked in the first vacant space I saw and made my way up the block, keeping an eye out for a newspaper box. Juniper Grove still had the old metal newspaper dispensers, even though all they ever held was the *Post* and a freebie classified ads paper.

Spotting one on the other side of the block, I stepped off the curb and waited for a car to pass. It slowed as it came closer, the passenger inspecting me as though I were a questionable salami hanging in a deli. My hair was a bit windblown, but nothing shocking, and maybe I'd indulged in one too many pastries, but *really*.

I dug for the quarters in my pocket and was about to drop them into the box's slot when I froze. There I was, front-page news in the *Post*. Standing in the doorway of my house, a haggard scowl on my face. No wonder that car had slowed. I looked like a crackpot—at best. I contemplated grabbing all the copies in the box, but my sensible self won out. I took one, folded it under my arm, and set out for Holly's Sweets.

The bakery was bustling, enabling me to hover unnoticed behind the crowd of customers. After a minute, curiosity got the better of me. Leaning on the back wall, I opened the paper, holding it close to my face. As bad as the photograph was, the caption was worse: "Rachel Stowe, the current homeowner of 504 Finch Hill Road, declined an offer to explain the circumstances surrounding the discovery of George Foster's body."

I puffed out my cheeks. *Declined an offer*. So that was an offer, was it? Knocking on my door late at night and shoving a camera in my face? If I, a relative newcomer to town with no connection to the old crime, could be treated so unfairly by the local press, what fibs had the paper told about Julia? Or Holly? No wonder those two disliked Newsome.

I glanced up. Holly had noticed me at the back of the shop and was tipping her head, as tactfully as one could do such things in public, toward one of the customers, a fifty-something man perusing the fruit tarts in the display case.

"Mr. Ventura," she called, holding out a bag. "Your scone."

The customer's gaze rose from the tarts to Holly. He pushed his glasses back up his nose, paid her, and made his way to the door.

I followed.

Holly being busy, I needed to make use of my time while I waited for things to calm down. Trailing Ventura down the sidewalk, I tried to come up with an opening line—a legitimate reason to introduce myself and ask him about George Foster. But he wasn't the mayor, someone I'd naturally want to meet. He was the town attorney. Then I realized I held the reason in my hand. The newspaper. I'd been dragged into this mess, hadn't I?

I quickened my steps until I was alongside him. "Mr. Ventura?"

"Yes?" he said, maintaining his rapid pace.

"I'm Rachel Stowe." I held out my hand.

Recognition flickered across his face. He shook my hand but kept moving. "What can I help you with?"

"I'd like to ask you a couple questions."

"Legal advice?"

"Possibly."

At last he came to a stop. "Town offices," he said. Rather needlessly, as the glass door in front of us bore the words "Juniper Grove Town Hall."

"Do you have a moment?" I asked.

"A couple minutes is all," he said, opening the door for me. "Straight ahead, first door on the left."

His office door was open, but I stepped to the side and waited for Ventura to enter first. It was a small but comfortable-looking office, though sparsely decorated. The two framed paintings on the wall were town-supplied, judging by their blandness, and the only personal touches were several photo frames propped on a narrow bureau along one wall.

Ventura gestured at a wooden chair in front of his desk. "Take a seat. Hope you don't mind if I have my breakfast while we talk."

"Not at all."

"So . . ." He reached into the bag and extracted a scone. "Rachel Stowe."

"You've heard of me."

"Anyone who gets the *Post* has by now, I imagine." He paused to take a bite of his scone and then went on, alternately talking and chewing. "Are you considering legal action?"

"Do you think I should?"

"You would never win."

"Then why did you ask?"

"I thought that was why you're here."

"The paper's photographer came to my door late last night, and I didn't give him permission to—"

"Did you open your door?"

"Of course."

He shrugged and took another bite of scone. "I'm sorry," he said, his mouth full. "Avoid Jillian Newsome. Most of us do."

"It's she who needs to avoid me."

"She's not going to do that." He studied the scone clutched between his fingers. "Mind your own business and you'll be fine."

"What does *that* mean?"

"Even better, tell Newsome she's intimidating you by coming to your house at night. Tell her you're afraid of her. Start setting up your defense."

"For what?"

"Your friend Holly Kavanagh makes the best pastries. We're lucky to have her, particularly in her prime spot downtown."

"She's very talented." Ventura was riveted to his scone. I sat back in my seat, waiting for him to take another bite. But instead of eating, he studied me, giving his gray beard a thoughtful scratch. Feeling uneasy, as though I had been threatened but couldn't put a finger on how, I returned to the subject of pastries. "Her cream puffs are the best I've ever had."

"I'll have to try them." He smiled a rather joyless smile, all mouth muscles and no emotion, his bulb of a nose broadening along with his lips. "Two other businesses vied for that spot on Main Street, did you know that? Holly lucked out somehow. She must have had a supporter on the Board of Trustees. I sure hope he stays a supporter."

I heard a rustle behind me followed by a knock on the open door.

"Tom, have you got a moment?" a man said, poking his head into the office. He glanced my way. "I'm sorry, I didn't mean to interrupt."

"No, we're finished here," Ventura said, ungraciously suggesting I leave.

"Douglas McDermott," the man said, his hand extended.

"Mr. Mayor," I replied, giving his hand a shake. "Pleased to meet you. Rachel Stowe." His youth took me by surprise. This dark-haired mayor was thirty-five years old, tops.

He leaned against the doorjamb. "*The* Rachel Stowe?"

I rolled my eyes. "That newspaper . . ."

McDermott's laughter echoed in the almost-bare office. "I shouldn't laugh, but we've all been there. Don't let it bother you."

"Jillian Newsome implied that I knew something about George Foster but refused to be forthcoming. How could that not bother me?"

McDermott's expression changed and his voice became serious. "Newsome walks a fine legal line. One of these days she's going to cross it. Or if we're lucky, she'll move to Denver or Colorado Springs first, in search of new and bigger prey. In the meantime, try not to worry about it."

Ventura cleared his throat and dropped what was left

of his scone into the bag. My signal to exit. But I had one more question. "Mr. Ventura," I said, rising from my chair, "how did you know Holly Kavanagh is my friend? The news article doesn't mention her, and you and I have never met before."

Ventura's deer-in-the-headlights look lasted a fraction of a second. He recovered quickly. "Holly must have told me."

Clearly, that was nonsense. "She tells you the names of her friends?"

He removed his glasses before he spoke. "Lady, I honestly don't remember, but I need to get to work."

In my peripheral vision I saw McDermott watching Ventura. If I had to guess, there was tension between the two men. Mistrust, even. Though that may have been wishful thinking on my part because I didn't want to believe that two of the top men in town government were shifty—or worse. I'd already made up my mind about Ventura, but I needed McDermott to be a good guy, a counterforce to the devious town attorney.

"It was nice meeting you both," I said. Turning to leave, I took a last quick look around the room and caught sight of a photograph in one of the frames. A recent one, judging by how little Ventura and Gilroy had changed since it had been taken. Fishing gear in hand, they were standing on a riverbank, grinning broadly as though they were the best of chums enjoying the best of times. Ventura looked out of place, with an embroidered handkerchief in his pocket and—of all things—a glass of wine in his hand. Gilroy looked like he belonged in the open spaces. "You're fishing partners with Chief Gilroy? I just met him." I twisted back. "You know, George Foster's body in my backyard. That sort of thing tends to bring the police."

Now McDermott was watching me, no doubt puzzled by my attitude toward Ventura.

What bothered me more than Ventura trying to get me to back off my questions, to go back to Finch Hill Road and ignore what was going on in my own backyard, was his vague threats—not just against me, but against Holly and her bakery.

"Have a good day," he said, that oily grin back on his face. "Say hello to Holly for me. Will I be seeing you both at the Farmers' Market Festival tomorrow?"

He seemed intent on mocking me. But threats and mockery, far from being weapons of power, were expressions of fear. Ventura was scared. "Oh, absolutely. We have every intention of being there."

CHAPTER 6

Heading back to Holly's Sweets, my attention was focused on the newspaper box ahead, which I soon judged to be empty. That meant the *Post* had sold out early and I could expect more stares. Contemplating this, I quite literally ran into Belinda Almond, putting a dent in the pastry box in her hands.

"I am so sorry," I said, steadying her with my hands. She was such a wisp of a woman, it was a wonder I hadn't sent her careening to the sidewalk. Even in heels she was at least two inches shorter than my five foot seven, and she was willowy, with small, neat fingers—which were now appraising her pink Holly's Sweet box for damage. "Did I ruin anything?"

"I don't think so. It's hard to ruin pastries, isn't it? Squished or not, they taste the same."

A woman after my own heart. I gave her exquisitely tailored navy skirt suit a quick appraisal. No damage there, thank goodness. "I'm Rachel Stowe, by the way."

There was a little hiccup in time—just a fraction of a second—before she returned the greeting. "I'm Belinda Almond. Nice to meet you."

"I have a feeling you've seen this." I raised my copy of the *Post*. Best to come right out with it.

She grimaced. "I did, I'm sorry. I keep meaning to cancel that thing. The problem is, there's no other paper in town. It looks like you got the Jillian Newsome treatment."

"I was foolish enough to open my own front door. Do you know Newsome?"

She cocked a well-plucked eyebrow. "I've had my conflicts with her. She makes a lasting impression."

"What do you mean?"

"Once you meet her, you never want to meet her again. Not that you necessarily have a choice."

Had Newsome learned of Belinda's affair with George and put it in the paper? I'd have to check with Holly on that. "It sounds like you made the news the same way I did, just minding your own business."

She nodded. "And made to look like I wasn't."

"I'm sorry. Can I ask . . . ?"

"Just ask around town. Ask about Belinda Almond, the home breaker. It's all a lie, but a lie gets halfway around the world before the truth puts its pants on—isn't that what they say?" Her voice carried the anger she no doubt felt for being exposed as George Foster's fling. As if to compensate for her bitter tone, she smiled.

"I don't like gossip. It's usually the opposite of fact." Something about this woman made me wonder if the gossip about her was wrong. Had Julia heard of George's affair with her from his own lips? Or had Jillian Newsome spread the rumor for her own purposes?

"Thank you, that's very kind. In this case, gossip *is* the opposite of fact."

I could no longer conceal what I knew—what I'd

heard—about Belinda. "Are you . . . I mean . . . well, talking about George Foster?"

Belinda's eyes narrowed. "You *do* know who I am."

"I didn't hear your name until yesterday, and this whole mess came up." I raised the paper again.

"Then you don't have to ask about me around town, do you? Did you run into me on purpose?"

"Of course not! Belinda, I'm new to Juniper Grove, and believe me, I have no preconceptions about anyone in this town, including you."

Her expression softened. She appeared to be considering what I'd said, trying to decide whether or not to snub me and move on. "You know something?" she said at last. "I met George Foster once in my entire life. It was at a benefit party for the library about a month before he disappeared, and his wife was at home sick. Foster was drunk, and he came on to me. I was trying to be nice. I should have slapped him. Just before I pushed him away, a photographer snapped a photo of us. Next thing you know, I'm having an affair with him."

"That's awful." If Belinda was telling the truth, her affair with George was a total fabrication of the *Post*. But why? To sell papers? True, Belinda might have been an easy target. Her makeup was overdone for Juniper Grove—red lipstick, blush, eye shadow. Was it as simple as that? She fit the *Post*'s adulteress template and Newsome liked her news tabloid-esque? It was outrageous.

"I'd never met him before, and George was just being a stupid, drunk man. We never saw each other again. So how do I put the jack-in-the-box back in the box?"

"Did the *Post* accuse you of having an affair?"

"They suggested as much in a caption to the photo."

"Have you thought about suing them?"

"This was seven years ago, Rachel. There's nothing to be done now. Besides, they didn't blatantly accuse me. You've seen how that works."

"Have you ever talked to Julia Foster?"

"Heavens, no. I'm sure she believes the paper. Most people do."

"There must be people who don't."

"I have some good friends here. They know the truth of what happened. But I also have some enemies. Just look at Holly Kavanagh over there, shooting daggers at me."

I followed Belinda's gaze across the street to where Holly was standing outside her shop. When I did, Holly waved me over, urgency in her body language. "I think she's shooting daggers at me. I was in her bakery earlier and was supposed to come back."

"Oh." Chagrined, Belinda tugged the strap of her blue-dyed leather purse higher up on her shoulder. The woman had expensive tastes. "You must think I'm paranoid."

"Are you going to be at the Farmers' Market Festival?"

"I might."

"I'll be there. Grab me if you see me. We'll have a coffee."

"Sounds good." Belinda smiled—this time a genuine rather than strained reaction—and said goodbye, heading down the sidewalk with her prized pastries.

I darted across the street to Holly, debating what to say to her about Belinda, but Holly had news that couldn't wait. She latched on to my arm and pulled me close to the bakery, her eyes dodging this way and that.

"Holly, for goodness' sake."

"Shh. You'll never believe it." Her eyes again scanned the sidewalk. "When I'm in the back of the bakery, I can hear what people say out front. Peter set up a monitor last month so we wouldn't miss a customer."

"Who did you hear?"

"Joe Smith and Jillian Newsome." Her lips pressed firmly together, Holly nodded with a you-heard-me-right look on her face. "They left five minutes ago. I waited until I was sure they'd walked far away."

"Who's watching the bakery?"

"Peter."

It was my turn to latch on to Holly's arm. I pulled her inside the bakery and around the counter, Peter smiling indulgently at us, then pulled her into the back, where I could be sure we wouldn't be overheard. "Tell me."

"Newsome asked Smith who was paying him to write those notes."

"You're joking."

"That's confirmation he's the note writer, if we had any doubt. But that means Newsome didn't arrange this stunt. Someone else did."

"Then why is she involved? How did she find out about Smith?"

"I bet Smith contacted her, and she was more than willing to help out. Scandal sells papers. He thanked her for her—get this—'assistance' and said his boss would be appreciative."

"Do you know if he's still at the B&B?"

"At least until tonight. He's meeting Newsome there. He said, and I quote, 'I'm far from done with this.' She asked him what that meant, and he wouldn't answer her. A few seconds later someone else came in the door and they stopped talking."

I tried to sort my thoughts, my mind coughing up question after question. "Holly, this may be bigger than we originally thought. Someone planned this thoroughly and cared about the plan enough to pay someone to carry it out. You don't go to that trouble for a prank."

Holly shivered. "What worries me is what he meant by 'far from done.'"

"That does it. Who's this Joe Smith? We need to find out. Do you know anyone who can trace an out-of-state license plate?"

"Trace a plate? I bake scones for a living," Holly said with a chuckle.

"We can't ask the Juniper Grove PD."

"Hardly." Deep in thought, Holly began to smooth her ponytail over one shoulder, a habit I'd noticed on first meeting her.

"Who then? Between you, me, and Julia, we must know someone. It's that six degrees thing. Someone knows someone, and that person knows someone else, and so on."

Holly dropped her hair. "I'm drawing a blank. Are we sure Joe Smith lives out of state?"

That burst my bubble. "No, we're not. I'm only guessing."

"Do you have those four plate numbers?"

"On my cell phone."

I started pacing the floor—my own deep-thoughts habit—the glazed concrete echoing my steps. All right, then. Someone had paid Joe Smith to write anonymous notes, but I was sure Smith had a stake in the matter. He'd told Newsome that *he* was far from done, and that sounded personal. Smith was a man with a grievance. Only an aggrieved man would pepper the town with notes he knew would brew serious trouble.

I stopped my pacing and wheeled back to Holly. "Did Newsome call Smith by any other name?"

"She called him Joe."

"Did she seem to know him? Or did she treat him like a stranger?"

Holly thought back. "She talked to him like he had a lot of information he wasn't telling her. I don't think she knew him."

"I wonder if our Mr. Smith is lying about being paid. I think this could be his own vendetta and he's using the mercenary angle to protect his identity."

"Which is?"

"Does the library have copies of the *Juniper Grove Post* going back seven years?"

Holly lit up. "Yes! Brilliant! Microfiche."

"Joe Smith, my cream puffs," I crowed. "He was involved in the Foster-Dillard case—or related to someone involved. How old did you say he was?"

"Early twenties."

"So he was in his mid-teens when the bank theft happened." That narrowed it down. I now had a strong suspicion who Joe Smith was, but I needed to confirm it. "Do you have to go back to the bakery?"

"Yeah, Peter hates it up front. Call me if you find out?"

Five minutes later I was seated in front of the library's sole microfiche machine, searching copies of the *Post* going back to the day of the bank theft and disappearance of Dillard and Foster. For the most part the news articles were appalling, filled with innuendo and unfounded accusations. Pretty much what I expected.

Gilroy, in particular, took a lot of heat in the accounts, with reporters openly wondering why Juniper Grove had hired a failed Fort Collins detective to be their new chief. Just when they needed him most, he'd failed again. "What failure?" I said under my breath. That was yet another matter to explore.

Though he and Hammond had found Dillard's body, which was quite a feat, considering its location—jammed between rocks in a wilderness area—neither of them was given a word of credit. The big trophy, Foster's body, eluded them.

Hammond, the underling, escaped most of the scathing remarks. Not so Gilroy. As I read the articles, I wondered why Gilroy had chosen to stay in Juniper Grove, so vicious were the comments about his qualifications to be chief. Oddly, Tom Ventura had stood up for him. The *Post* quoted him as saying the town would hire him again without hesitation. Well, they were fishing buddies.

Julia was questioned in one of the articles. Ambushed at her home was more like it. Much was made of her slamming the door in the reporter's face. "What does Julia Foster know about her husband's disappearance?" a reporter asked. I could have smacked the microfiche machine.

In the next issue of the paper, I found what I believed was my answer. In the wake of Mitch Dillard's death, his wife, Deborah, and his son, age sixteen, were moving back to Utah, where they had family. "George Foster murdered my dad," Aiden Dillard was quoted as saying. "And one of these days I'm coming back to prove it."

Aiden had done just that. He'd come back. As Joe Smith.

CHAPTER 7

"Aiden Dillard wrote those notes?" Julia said. She appeared pained but not terribly surprised by the revelation. "That poor misguided boy."

She handed me a cup of coffee and I followed her to her living room, where we sat in a pair of armchairs flanking the large picture window that overlooked her front porch. The dazzling afternoon sun was behind us, on the other side of the house, but the day's warm hours had given Julia's house a closed-in, hothouse feeling. More like August than September.

"Aiden's not a boy anymore," I reminded her.

"No, he's a young man, but I always thought he was very hurt when he found out his father stole that money and planned to leave him and his mother. He was almost . . . damaged by it." She turned to gaze out the window. "Still, I don't understand what he thinks he's going to achieve."

"He may not be thinking that clearly. Or thinking that far ahead."

"Oh, well." She sighed and turned back to me, a faint smile on her lips. "It's good to know it's Aiden. I can understand it now."

"Don't take it lightly, Julia. He's not a teenager anymore. He's a grown man with a serious grudge, and in his own words, he's not finished."

"I don't know what else he thinks he can do."

I paused to take a long, savoring sip of coffee, carefully considering my next words. I didn't want to frighten Julia, but she seemed oblivious to one glaring possibility. "I think it's possible Aiden killed George. He blamed him for his father's death."

Julia was quiet, her expression thoughtful as she mulled over my words.

"He has more reason than anyone else," I added.

"That we know of," Julia said softly.

"Agreed. We need to know more."

Julia seemed to breathe a sigh of relief. She smiled, the skin around her brown eyes crinkling. "I thought you might decide to quit after you found out who wrote the notes. You only agreed to help with that."

"That was before we found your husband."

"Thank you," she said with a small nod of her head. "I think Jillian Newsome is going to make it look like I had something to do with George's death."

"Not on my watch." I scooted to the edge of the armchair, ready to stand. "What do we do next?"

"You should tell Chief Gilroy what you found out about Aiden."

"I will. And you need to be careful. Aiden might blame you as much as he blamed George."

"The *Juniper Grove Post* made it easy for him to hate both of us."

"And don't forget Aiden is working with Jillian Newsome." The day was hot, my coffee was hot. I set my cup on a side table, stood, and looked out over Julia's porch and garden, half expecting to see Newsome or one of her photographers on the lawn. My mind flitted from Newsome to Aiden and on to Chief Gilroy, the former Fort Collins detective. What had brought him to Juniper Grove? "Julia, do you remember when Chief Gilroy was hired?" I asked, turning back from the window.

"Yes, I do."

"Who hired him?"

"The Board of Trustees, on Tom Ventura's recommendation. He's the town attorney."

"Yes, I remember. Holly said he got one of the notes too. I met him this morning."

"Did you?"

"There's something fishy about him. Speaking of which, he and Gilroy are fishing buddies."

"Are they? I could never understand the attraction."

"To Gilroy?"

"To fishing."

"What was the board's vote on the hiring?"

"Unanimous. Everyone was thrilled that we finally found someone with experience. Our old chief was incompetent."

"That's what the *Post* calls Gilroy. Incompetent."

"More nonsense."

"Your husband thought Gilroy was a liar. Remember the piece of paper in the box?"

"It was George who was the liar," Julia said. "He lied about everything under the sun, and he was always scribbling things."

"Like what?"

"Mostly letters to the editor or ideas for letters to the editor. He complained about everything all the time."

"The issue of the *Post* I read, the one with Aiden in it, said Gilroy was a failed cop. Do you know why?"

Julia sat forward, eager to take on the subject. "I know exactly why. Politics. Gilroy ruffled the wrong feathers in Fort Collins. He refused to bow down to people in positions of power. He's a straight arrow, and a lot of powerful people don't like straight arrows."

"What did he do?"

"He arrested the mayor's wife for drunk driving."

"Holy cow."

"The mayor was in a car behind his wife's car. After Chief Gilroy pulled his wife over, he drove up, got out, and asked the chief to forget it all and let him drive his wife home. Gilroy wouldn't allow it, and it came out later that this wasn't the wife's first DUI. The mayor and his friends started a whisper campaign against Gilroy—how he'd blundered here and there and had lost the confidence of the people on his team."

As I pondered this intriguing news, I realized that Julia might not have the facts straight, that this story about Gilroy might be one more bit of unsubstantiated gossip. "How do you know this for certain?"

"When the Board of Trustees suggested hiring Gilroy, I went online and read the transcript of a Fort Collins city meeting. It was all in there."

I wasn't convinced. "But who was saying what?"

"The mayor wanted to fire Gilroy and replace him with someone who supposedly had more experience, but city residents were behind Gilroy a hundred percent. They knew the truth."

"Would the mayor be so openly political?"

Julia looked at me as though I'd just rolled out of a cabbage patch.

"You're right, silly question."

"That mayor is long gone now," Julia added. "The scandals finally caught up with him. And Juniper Grove got a—"

"Straight arrow," I finished.

"Precisely."

"With pale blue eyes."

Julia frowned. "You and Holly. That's not why I like him. Though I'm not so old I can't still notice a handsome man when I see one." She pointed a long, thin finger at me. "You're not immune either. I saw the way you looked at him when he was in your kitchen."

"Oh, please."

I suddenly had the strangest feeling that I was being watched, framed as I was by Julia's window. I moved away from it, working the kinks out of my legs. I *had* to get back to walking. Forty-three was way too young to feel this stiff, and if I didn't get back to exercising, I'd have to go up yet another size in clothing. "I'm going back to work."

"You know what I'm talking about," Julia insisted.

I grabbed my coffee cup and strode for the kitchen, my friend and her absurd imaginings on my heels.

"He's the right age for you," she said, not letting up. "A handful of years older."

"And a handful of pounds thinner," I said with a grin, setting my cup in her sink.

"He's four inches taller than you."

I stared. "What does that . . . ?" *Oh no, you're not pulling me into this again.* Julia had been trying to pair me off with someone, anyone, since I'd first moved to Juniper Grove. A month ago it was our single mail carrier. A nice enough man, but we had zero in common. "I really have to go. If you hear from Holly, tell her what I found out. She was too busy to talk when I checked back at the bakery."

I made it out in the nick of time, Julia launching into her "my single nephew" speech just as my feet hit her porch. I turned, waved, and hightailed it to my house.

After a quick sandwich, I headed out the back door for my garage, my eyes drawn once again to the bright yellow crime tape in my backyard. For no earthly reason that I could see, it remained—and probably would until I took it down. The police hadn't been back since I'd found Foster's body. I hurried into the house for scissors, came back out again, and then unceremoniously cut the tape in several places, leaving tape tails waving in the wind.

I drew near the hole, wondering how I'd fill it in. The digger had flung soil from the hole all about the yard rather than pile it up so I could easily push it back in. Murderers weren't known for their neatness. And Gilroy had thought I was planting a tree. I chuckled to myself.

The grass where Foster had lain was stained brown with dried blood. If it didn't rain soon, I'd come out with a bucket of water and wash it away. It made me a little sick to my stomach to look at it, and I didn't want Julia to have to see it again. Walking over to my small cherry tree, I slid one scissor blade under a knot of crime tape wound about its trunk, cut, and stuffed the tape in my jeans. Casting my eyes over the scene, I noticed a small white stick near my lilac bushes.

On closer inspection, I could see it was a partially smoked cigarette. Someone had discarded it after only a few puffs. No one, and I mean no one, smoked in my backyard. In fact, no one I knew smoked, period, and since I'd been in Juniper Grove I'd seen a grand total of two smokers, both teenagers. I bent down and was about to pick it up when I realized it might be evidence. It was possible the killer had been puffing away on a cigarette while he waited for Foster. "This is . . . this is so . . . ," I sputtered, "incompetent!" How could three police officers and a forensics unit leave evidence behind?

Now I really did have to talk to Gilroy—and fast. He or one of his sloppy officers needed to come back to my house and pick that thing up. And then I'd tell them about Aiden Dillard. Not that I had any confidence my discovery would mean anything to the Juniper Grove Police Department.

Fifteen minutes after calling the station, Chief Gilroy himself was in my backyard, a plastic bag and tweezers in hand. "You cut the tape," he said, slipping on a pair of gloves.

"Is that a problem?"

"No, we were done."

Choosing to keep mum, I bit back a sarcastic *Obviously not*. Gilroy was embarrassed enough without me adding to his discomfort.

He crouched next to the cigarette. "Is this the first you've seen this?"

"Yes, but I haven't really looked around my yard until now. Not in the daylight, anyway." Was it Aiden's? I wondered. Was he the smoker? I couldn't believe it was some teenager who didn't even know me.

Gilroy tweezed the cigarette and dropped it into the evidence bag.

"Do you think the killer was smoking that?" I asked.

Gilroy peered up at me. "This wasn't here last night."

"Are you sure?"

He stood, grunting a little with the effort. "We went

over every inch of your back and front yard."

Nevertheless, Gilroy began to walk the yard, his eyes to the ground. He seemed positive he and his men hadn't missed any evidence the first time around, and now I was tempted to believe him. The more I thought about it, that cigarette, a white stick in a field of green, had been eye-catching. Missing it would have been blindness, not incompetence.

"Aiden Dillard wrote those anonymous notes," I said to Gilroy's back. He turned. "My friends and I found out. He's staying at the Lilac Lane B&B."

"Mitch Dillard's son?" he asked.

"That's him."

He shook his head, told me to stay out of it, and went on with his search.

You're welcome, I thought.

As Gilroy continued to walk, I brainstormed reasons for that cigarette to have ended up in my fenced yard. I came up with three feasible scenarios. First, Aiden had returned to the scene of his triumph—whether or not he'd killed Foster—and deliberately left a piece of evidence. A risky and pointless thing to do. Second, a cigarette-smoking neighbor or thrill seeker, looking to find the place where the famous George Foster had finally met his end, dropped it. That thought made me want to contact a home-security company. Or third, someone who didn't like Gilroy was trying to make him and his police force look bad. Again.

CHAPTER 8

That evening I drove back to the Lilac Lane B&B, hoping to catch sight of Aiden Dillard, a.k.a. Joe Smith. Newsome knew my face, but Aiden probably didn't—unless he recognized me from the paper—so I figured I could park across the street, in the dark between streetlights, and sit without catching his attention. Half an hour later, I realized the folly of my plan. I had no idea where Aiden was. Maybe he'd made an early night of it or even left town. Or maybe he was at a restaurant or downtown brewpub, carousing with Jillian Newsome.

I was about to start the Forester when I saw a silver SUV pull in front of the B&B. Two doors, front and back, opened, and two men exited the car and mounted the front steps. In the bright light of the entrance, they paused. Tom Ventura stuck out his hand and Aiden Dillard grasped it, giving it a firm and friendly shake.

I stared, unbelieving. "This is dirty," I said under my breath. "Something is really dirty."

Before I could grab my phone and take a photo, the men had moved on, Aiden into the B&B, and Ventura back to the SUV. I was rooted to my car seat, not knowing where to go or what to do next. I had thought that Ventura, who supposedly had been shocked to find an anonymous note on his door yesterday morning, was a victim—like Julia,

Holly, and the others. But it was all a ruse. His note had been added to the others as cover. He was in on it. Whatever *it* was.

What were he and Aiden up to? They had to have more in mind than just stirring up bad memories. Had one of them killed George Foster? Maybe Aiden had, and Ventura was helping him by concealing or muddying the evidence. More frightening than that thought was that I had no clue who was on their side. Their circle of friends, and partners in crime, had to be broader than I yet knew. The only people I could trust were Holly and Julia. Even Belinda Almond was now on my Treat with Caution List.

I decided to make a stop at Holly's house on my way home. I needed to tell someone what I'd just seen, and I didn't want to get Julia worked up so late in the day. She suffered from insomnia, and tales about killer attorneys wouldn't help with her sleep.

Driving down Main Street, I saw Holly and her husband talking to Officer Hammond outside the bakery door. It was unpleasant business, I could tell, not a happy, chance meeting. Frustration on his face, Peter was gesturing at the bakery, and Hammond, grim-faced, hands on his hips, was listening politely.

I parked in the first open spot and marched to where Holly was leaning against her shop, her arms folded and eyes downcast.

"Holly?" I called.

She looked up. Her arms dropped to her sides. "Rachel, I can't believe it. We've had a break-in." Her voice was rough from crying and her eyes were red-rimmed and puffy.

"When did this happen?"

"I closed up two hours ago, and I came back, just now, to check on the chocolate. I thought . . . and the festival's tomorrow. What am I going to do? All the pastries are ruined."

"Everything?"

"Everything." Holly wasn't the hysterical type. If she said everything, she meant it. She sniffed and turned her face from Peter and Officer Hammond. "In the back of the shop, where I was storing all the pastries I was going to sell tomorrow. They might have missed a whole four or five scones, but . . ." She sniffed again and rubbed the back of her hand against her nose. "All destroyed for no reason."

"What about the front of the shop?" I cupped my hands around my eyes and peered into the bakery.

"They didn't touch the front. I think with all the foot traffic on this street they knew someone might see them."

"Do you have any idea who it was?"

"Not the faintest. We've never had any trouble before. None of the store owners on Main Street have." She leaned in close. "And I don't think Hammond has a clue how to proceed. I asked him if he was going to look for fingerprints and his answer was to ask me if we had closed-circuit TV. No one on this street has cameras."

"I don't suppose your voice monitor can record sound," I said.

"I wish."

Camera in hand, Officer Underhill walked up to Officer Hammond, spoke briefly, and strode to the bakery door.

"Reinforcements," I said.

Holly shrugged. "Lot of good that will do."

"Give them a chance."

"Come take a look. It's unbelievable."

The back of the bakery was as bad as I'd feared. Dough, fruit fillings, icing—everywhere. On the walls, on the countertops, on the range tops. Fortunately, at least on first look, pastry damage was the only damage. I'd expected to see dented ovens and smashed glass at least, but it was just pastry. Loads of it. Someone had had a fine old time.

I felt my temper rise. Such senseless destruction. And Holly had so been looking forward to the Farmers' Market Festival tomorrow. It was a major event in Juniper Grove. Every vegetable grower, quilter, brewmaster, and culinary artist in town would be there to hawk their wares. There was no better opportunity for Holly to spread the word about her treats to the few slackers who didn't yet know she was the best pastry chef in northern Colorado.

My heart sank as I looked about. If I rolled up my sleeves and pitched in, and some of Holly's and Peter's friends did the same, maybe we could slap the place into shape by the end of the weekend. She might even be able to open on Monday.

Knowing Hammond and Underhill were still at work, I resisted the temptation to start the cleanup. The officers disappeared with Peter out the back door, and Holly, after looking at the back door again, trudged over to where I was standing, looking a little brighter than she had a few minutes ago. "It looks like they picked the lock," she said. "We'll need to call a locksmith, but they didn't bust the door, break any windows, or spray-paint the building."

"Thank goodness."

"I thought I must have missed something when I first looked, but I just looked again. Peter's checking the parking lot. But it looks like the only damage is here." She spread her hands. "It's a royal mess, but it's not permanent."

I put my arm around her shoulder. "You'll get through this. I'll help. Julia will too, I'll bet," I said with a grin. "You know what a wiz she is at cleaning. Just watch us."

"No. Positively no." She vehemently shook her head. "This is what I have insurance for. You will not touch a thing, and neither will I."

The three men reentered the bakery, Officer Underhill snapping photos every two steps. As unlikely as it was that a photo of crushed croissants on a metal countertop offered any clues to the culprits, I bit my tongue, refusing to comment. Holly didn't need to know that I shared her pessimism when it came to the Juniper Grove Police Department. Leaving Underhill to his work, Peter began to examine the refrigerator contents, opening containers, sniffing and testing, and probably wondering if he should toss it all for safety's sake.

"Does your insurance cover this?" I whispered.

"It covers vandalism of all kinds, including cleanup thereof. I'm hiring a cleaning crew first thing tomorrow."

Admittedly, I was relieved. The prospect of spending an entire weekend with a towel and mop wasn't appealing.

"I also have to call the festival committee first thing and let them know there won't be a Holly's Sweets table."

I sighed and looked at my friend. What could I say? "People still know you're best."

"There's always next September."

"I'm sorry about this, Holly," said Officer Hammond as he made his way over. He slipped his notebook back into his uniform, removed his hat, and gave his head a scratch. "And you're certain nothing was taken?"

"Nothing I can see. It's pretty much just . . . pastry mess."

Hammond smiled. His slightly buck teeth contributed to his friendly, open look, I decided. Perfection, even in teeth, was intimidating.

"One piece of good news," he said. "It doesn't look like they touched anything out back. Peter and I gave it a thorough search. Officer Underhill is going to dust for prints, but I'm not hopeful."

"Neither am I," Holly replied.

"We'll talk to other shop owners on the street, see if they noticed anything. Whoever it was came in the back." Hammond tossed his chin in the direction of the back door. "But we don't know if they walked to the bakery, drove, or were let off. We don't know if it was one person, two, or more. But we're just getting started, so don't lose hope."

I decided to offer my two cents. If Hammond was anything like Gilroy, he'd grunt and ignore me, but I needed to speak up. "This looks to me like someone had two minutes in which to make the biggest mess they could—and ruin Holly's day at the festival tomorrow."

Scanning the pastry debris one more time, Hammond nodded thoughtfully and rubbed his chin. "A short-term goal, in other words."

"Otherwise," I asked, "why wouldn't they have destroyed some of the expensive equipment back here?"

Hammond turned to Holly. "Can you think of anyone who wanted to keep your bakery out of the festival that badly?"

"No," she said. "Not a soul. None of the other owners

would do this." The idea bewildered her. Holly had often spoken to me about the good relationships among Main Street shop owners. Once, she said, after the florist down the street suffered water damage from hail-broken skylights, the other owners pitched in to help, getting her back on her feet in twenty-four hours. Main Street, even in a town like Juniper Grove, where shops vied for a limited number of customers, was not cutthroat.

"Then could it be personal?" Hammond asked. "Someone who wanted to cause you trouble?"

"No," Holly said again. "Anyway, if someone really wanted to get me, why wouldn't they have destroyed the stove or refrigerator? They cost thousands."

"Thousands of dollars in damage means a bigger fine or even prison time if they're caught," Hammond said. "Especially with breaking and entering added on."

Holly ran her hand across her forehead. I could see that turning a suspicious eye to her neighbors was as wearying as contemplating the damage done to her shop.

"Well . . ." Hammond looked down at his shoes. He wanted to leave, I thought, but was reluctant to abandon Holly and Peter to the chaos around them and the sad knowledge that someone in their little town had disliked them or the bakery enough to hurt them in this way. "The chief will be out tomorrow morning. Will you or Peter be here?"

"Directing a cleaning crew, I hope. Tell Gilroy not to stir himself." With that, Holly walked off to join her husband, who was still digging into the fridge.

Hammond threw me a strained smile. "Chief Gilroy's looking into that cigarette you found."

Meaning *That explains why he isn't at the bakery.*

"What's he doing with it?"

"I don't know. He stared at it and took off. I've learned that usually means something."

Funny. To me Gilroy's stares were the product of arrogance, nothing more. I believed he and his officers had been diligent in their first search of my yard, but something wasn't up to snuff in the department. It was time to broach the subject—or poke the hornet's nest, depending on what happened next. "I keep hearing that Chief Gilroy made big mistakes in Fort Collins and that's why he came here."

A frown creased Hammond's brow.

"Jillian Newsome makes a point of saying it," I added.

Hammond gave me a sharp look. "And you believe her?"

"She's not trustworthy, I know that."

"Then?" He chuckled in disbelief. "Let me tell you something. Most people in Juniper Grove are good. They'll give you the shirts off their backs. But there are some—and Jillian Newsome is one of them—who like to spread rumors and trash reputations. Gilroy's been chief for more than seven years. What does that tell you?"

I wished now I hadn't said anything. I sounded like I enjoyed a bit of hearsay myself, though truth was I hated gossip.

"Rachel Stowe?" Slinging his camera strap over his shoulder, Officer Underhill walked up to our little circle. "I hear you found something in your backyard this morning."

Overhearing him, Holly came up beside me. "What's this?"

"I think it was left there deliberately," I said.

"You never know," Underhill said.

Noncommittal. Just like Gilroy. "Chief Gilroy was at my house earlier," I told Holly. "I found a cigarette in the backyard that wasn't there last night."

Holly's eyes widened. "You mean someone was in your yard after the police left?"

It took seeing Holly's reaction for me to fully grasp the danger I'd been in. And Julia, too. Someone had entered my fenced-in yard last night and dropped a cigarette twenty feet from my back door in the pitch black. No thrill-seeking neighbor or tourist would do that. It was either someone determined to put Gilroy to shame or—I shuddered at the thought—the killer or someone working with him.

CHAPTER 9

Though I'd lain awake most of the night listening for snapping twigs and other signs of an intruder in my backyard, I woke early the next morning, ate a large breakfast, and was in my car by nine o'clock. I'd been looking forward to the Farmers' Market Festival since moving to Juniper Grove. Fresh organic vegetables, neighborhood crafts, a special Farmers' Brew from Grove Coffee I'd heard a lot about. Sadly, there would be none of Holly's cream puffs, but my body was telling me to knock off the pastries for a while.

Anyway, Holly had said she would be there. *I'm going to ask questions and find out who did this*, was what she'd actually said. Peter, who wasn't much of a festival person, had said he would stay behind to supervise the cleanup at the bakery if Holly promised to enjoy herself—really enjoy herself and not grill their neighbors.

Holly and I planned to meet with Julia near the coffee tent at about ten o'clock. Meanwhile, I was going to check out the organic veggies, all while keeping an eye out for Tom Ventura, Jillian Newsome, and maybe even Aiden Dillard. The three of them were so bold, meeting one another at a downtown B&B, that I half expected to see them stroll arm in arm onto the festival grounds.

I was also on the lookout for Belinda Almond, hoping I'd find her before Julia arrived. I hadn't told Julia about running into Belinda, literally, and I didn't want to add to the stress my neighbor was under.

I cut across the fairgrounds and followed the aroma of fresh-brewed coffee to the coffee tent. After buying a cup of the fabled Farmers' Brew, I sat on an enameled steel bench beneath the shade of an ash tree. For a few minutes, the troubles of the past two days vanished. I felt at ease, and grateful once again that I'd found a home here. Grateful for my friends. Grateful for September blue skies, a cool breeze, and, curved around me like a velvet horseshoe, the foothills of the Rocky Mountains, so close I could almost touch them.

My moment of ease was cut short by Jillian Newsome, whose sudden appearance in front of me blocked my view of the mountains.

"Rachel, have you got a moment?" she asked, motioning at the bench. She sat before I could open my mouth.

"Good morning," I said as I went back to gazing at the scenery. "Don't you feel blessed to live here?"

The question seemed to stump her. "Um, I guess." She plucked a piece of lint from her black skirt and flicked it to the ground.

I raised my Styrofoam cup. "Have you tried the Farmers' Brew?"

"I'll get around to it. I wanted to ask you something."

And I've been wanting to ask you something. But for now I'm keeping quiet about what I know.

"First of all, Rachel, I'm sorry I surprised you at your door like that."

"Never mind."

"No, it was uncalled for."

"Just don't do it again, please."

"Listen, Rachel, what can you tell me about this cigarette you found yesterday?"

She was using my name repeatedly to bait me. A salesman's tactic. "How did you hear about that?"

"I'm in the newspaper business." She shot me a doughy, catlike smile.

That's not the business you're in, I wanted to say. But I was being rude. Realizing I was hunched over—posture was not my strong suit—I sat up straight and gave her the attention she deserved. "Listen, Jillian, you'll have to ask the police about anything to do with the Foster case."

She clicked her tongue. "I was hoping you could help me out."

"You know as much as I do, Jillian. Probably more."

She tilted her head my way. "I very much doubt that."

"I'll tell you something worth investigating, Jillian. My friend Holly Kavanagh had her bakery broken into last night."

"That's awful."

"It's never happened to her before. So I've been asking myself, why now?"

"And what answer are you giving yourself?"

"No answers, just possibilities."

"Care to share any?"

I shook my head. "I haven't had time to think them through. But I thought maybe if you wrote about the break-in, someone might recall seeing something yesterday and go to the police. Breaking and entering on Main Street is worth the *Post*'s attention."

"Not when there are scandals to uncover." Her eyes shifted to the coffee tent. "Mayor McDermott!" she called out, waving a hand.

McDermott acknowledged her with a smile then quickened his steps until he was inside the tent. "What scandals, Jillian?"

"I don't have any answers yet either, Rachel. You can read about it when I do."

"What if you're wrong, Jillian?"

She stood abruptly. "About what?"

"About anyone. What if you ruin a reputation?" Her eyes were riveted to the tent. I felt sorry for the mayor and insanely wanted to shout out a warning to him: *Run now*.

"Let's be specific. Who are you talking about?"

"We can start with Julia Foster."

Jillian threw back her head and laughed.

"You think making someone's life miserable is funny?" I asked. Infuriated, I got to my feet, trying hard not to spill my coffee, and positioned myself between Jillian and the tent. Over Newsome's shoulder I caught sight of Chief Gilroy and Officer Hammond deep in conversation, presumably over the beer bottles they were scrutinizing. So much for the cigarette inquiry. I returned my focus to Newsome.

"Rachel," she said, back to using my name, "you weren't in Juniper Grove back then. You need to know the facts before you make a presumption."

"Exactly what *I* was going to say, Jillian."

"There's something else you need to know. Nobody ever wins against a newspaper. It's like a bicycle versus a truck in a traffic accident." She jutted out her chin. "The paper is the truck."

She took off for the coffee tent. Ten seconds later, Juniper Grove's mayor came flying out the back of the tent. McDermott raced through a grassy field and then back onto the fairgrounds, cutting a zigzag pattern between craft tables as though he were avoiding sniper fire.

Unable to keep myself from laughing, I turned quickly from the tent—and straight into Julia. The force of our collision knocked the Styrofoam cup from my hands, sending a river of coffee down the front of my T-shirt.

"Rachel, I'm sorry!" Julia cried.

"No, it's me! I'm so clumsy!" In spite of the mess, I continued to laugh. At least the coffee had cooled before I'd dumped it all over myself.

Julia looked slightly bewildered. "I'm glad you have a sense of humor."

"It's just that I was laughing at something before, and . . ." I put my hand on her arm. "Never mind, it's an old shirt."

Julia relaxed. "What were you laughing at?"

"I shouldn't have laughed at her." I glanced over my shoulder at the coffee tent. No Jillian to be seen. "Jillian Newsome is full of herself, isn't she? I think she just threatened me with the power of the *Post*."

Julia's face grew troubled. "Why would she threaten you?"

"I wouldn't talk to her about the cigarette I found yesterday." In answer to Julia's puzzled look, I filled her in on the details of the cigarette in my backyard. "Gilroy is supposedly checking into it, though I don't know what he thinks he's going to discover. Anyway, Newsome found out about it and got a little touchy when I wouldn't give her details."

"What did she say to you?"

"It's not important, and I'm not letting that woman ruin my day. Have you seen Holly?"

But Julia, who didn't share my lighthearted view of the newspaper's editor in chief, wasn't so easily diverted. "You have to take Newsome seriously. If you anger her, she'll go after you. She's already gone after me, so I have nothing to lose by confronting her. But you do."

For the first time I saw how profoundly Jillian Newsome had affected my friend's life. I knew, of course, that Julia had been hurt by the *Juniper Grove Post*, but this? What Newsome might or might not like was determining Julia's actions. And that was wrong.

I recalled Newsome on the steps of the B&B with Aiden Dillard, and I badly wanted to tell Newsome I'd seen her there, in hopes that would cause her to use a little restraint in her dealings with others. In hopes she'd see it as a threat, actually. *Mess with Julia, and I talk.* Wisdom won out. "I have a feeling that Newsome won't wield the power she does now when everything comes out."

"Her meeting with Aiden Dillard?" Julia scoffed. "She'll claim it was part of her job as an editor and reporter."

"It's more than that. I haven't had a chance to tell you, but last night I saw Aiden Dillard with Tom Ventura on the steps of the B&B. They know each other."

Julia gaped. "Ventura? Why would he be talking to Aiden? How would he even know Aiden is in town?"

"For a while last night I wondered if Ventura had found out who'd written the note and tracked Aiden down, like we did, but I don't think so. They shook hands like friends. Ventura either knows what Aiden is up to or he's in on it with him." I hooked my arm around Julia's and started for the coffee tent. "Come on, let's find Holly."

Julia took a few steps then stopped cold. "Over there, by the canning supplies. Is that . . . ? I think it is."

I nodded. "Aiden Dillard."

"That young man. I should walk right up to him and tell him I know he wrote the notes and I want him to stop this foolishness and get on with his life."

The grandmother—this time the disciplinary grandmother—was again coming out in Julia.

"I've got a better idea," I said, handing her my empty cup. "You stay by the coffee tent and wait for Holly. I'm going to follow Aiden around the grounds and see who he talks to."

Julia looked disappointed. Grandmother or not, she loved a good hunt. "I suppose he knows my face too well."

"And don't go off by yourself anywhere."

I double-timed it across the fairgrounds until I was twenty feet directly behind Aiden, then measured my steps to his, making sure I drew no closer. As I trailed him, I stopped now and then at tables and tents, feigning an interest in crocheted throws and jars of honey. If Aiden turned, I wanted to look like I was examining festival goods, not him.

Aiden strolled the grounds, pausing at tables, chatting with quiltmakers, and surveying the grounds every minute or so. He was no more interested in the crafts than I was. He was waiting for someone.

Aiden halted. I turned to reach for a jar of blackberry jam and lowered my head as if studying the label.

"That's organic," the jam maker said.

"Wonderful. How much?"

"Five dollars."

I dug into my jeans pocket, handed the man a bill, and stood gazing at the jar. While apparently—to anyone watching—mesmerized by the label, I took stock of the fairgrounds. Aiden was two tables to my right, Chief Gilroy and Officer Hammond had separated and were walking about the grounds, and Belinda Almond—at last I'd found her—was in a line for a donut near the coffee tent. Even Tom Ventura had made an appearance. Standing by a flagpole at one end of the field, looking bored stiff and hot as a potato in his long-sleeved business shirt, he was cleaning his glasses on his left sleeve. When he slipped them back on, he began to inspect the grounds, his head pivoting in increments, checking first one slice and then the next of festival pie.

I looked behind me, trying to see what Ventura was seeing, wondering if Julia and Holly were both in the coffee tent now. When I turned back, Aiden was gone. In that brief moment, he had disappeared. I looked to my left and right—no Aiden. I could only guess that he'd circled behind me and darted into one of the tents, and if he'd taken such evasive action, he knew I was watching him.

Thunder rumbled, announcing the arrival of a storm. Intent on following Aiden, I hadn't noticed the dark clouds scudding across the sky. We were about to get our first rain in almost four weeks.

"Not now," someone moaned.

"We need the moisture," came a reply.

"Not on my patchwork, we don't."

The jam maker began to stow his jars in cardboard

boxes, and at the table next to his, a woman gathered the ends of her tablecloth, using it as a giant sack to haul her homemade soaps to one of the tents.

My eyes swept over the grounds and back to Ventura, who now was standing open-mouthed, transfixed by the sight of something behind me.

I swung back. What was he looking at? Everyone had moved. Gilroy and Hammond were nowhere to be seen, Belinda had disappeared, Newsome was smiling at Aiden as she passed by him, giving him a nod, and I could see McDermott once more, this time by the organic vegetables. It was as though the field was a giant chessboard and the important chess pieces were in constant motion.

When I twisted back to Ventura, he too had disappeared.

"What is going on?" I said aloud.

"We're about to get rained on," the jam maker said.

"Right," I said, feeling foolish. How long had I been standing there, spinning this way and that?

Thunder rumbled again, louder this time, and the race to keep crafts and food from getting a soaking accelerated. But I was rooted in place, unable to shake the feeling that the answer to who killed George Foster had been right in front of me, if only I could have seen it.

I shook my head and set out for the coffee tent, jogging the last few steps as the clouds opened, ending our little drought. Julia and Holly found me, and we stood silently near the front of the tent, delighting in the scent of rain, listening as it tapped on the canvas.

Five minutes later the storm was over, though thunder still sounded in the distance.

"Careful, everyone," someone said. "Watch for

lightning out there."

"Where's my umbrella?" a woman said. "It was right here and now it's gone."

I stepped out of the tent and breathed deeply of the damp air.

"It's so fresh," Julia said, tilting her face to the sky. "We needed this."

All around us, people were emerging from the tents, sniffing the air like a pack of puppies. I caught sight of a woman wobbling her way around the quilting tent by clutching at the canvas. My first thought was she'd had too much craft beer, but now I could see that her face was contorted in fear. "Julia, Holly, look," I said, moving toward her.

The woman staggered to a stop and bent forward, hands on her knees. When she straightened, she let out a scream that echoed across the grounds.

CHAPTER 10

By the time I'd wrangled my way through the crowd, around the woman who had screamed and to the back of the quilting tent, Chief Gilroy and Officer Hammond were already there, crouched over Aiden Dillard. Gilroy had his fingers to Aiden's neck, checking for a pulse, but that was a formality. Aiden was on his back in the wet grass, staring with vacant eyes at the sky, a knitting needle in his neck.

"Who is he?" a woman said, her voice high and breathless.

"I can't believe it's another murder," a man said.

Officer Hammond stood and began to push the crowd back on all sides. "Clear the area, everyone. Away from the tent, but stay on the fairgrounds."

I couldn't bear another second looking at Aiden's face. I grabbed Julia and Holly and headed for the bench where I'd had my encounter with Jillian Newsome.

We sat quietly for several minutes, absorbed in our own thoughts, and watched as an ambulance bucked across the field toward the quilting tent.

Julia broke the silence. "Poor Aiden. That poor, sad boy. What a waste."

After he'd terrorized her by spreading his notes around town and conspired with the *Juniper Grove Post* to dredge up the horror of seven years ago, Julia was forgiving enough to say that. I put an arm around her and rested my head on her shoulder. "I was watching him but lost track," I said. "I think he knew I was following."

"Whatever Aiden was up to, it wasn't going to end well," Holly said. "Think how bitter he was. He traveled here from Utah to get back at people who had nothing to do with his father's death. Besides, if anyone other than Aiden is to blame for this, it's Mitch Dillard. What he did to his own son was a disgrace. Stealing from the bank, deserting him." She shook her head sadly.

"The police are going to question us," I said, sitting straight. "When they're done, let's go to my house. We'll order pizza and talk. I need to work this out."

"There's still the matter of who killed my husband," Julia said, nodding her agreement. "And I'd rather not be alone right now."

"We also need to find out what Newsome is up to," Holly said.

"And who broke into your bakery, because I'm betting it's connected," I added. I saw the county coroner's van drive onto the fairgrounds, a patrol car behind it. "That must be Officer Underhill. How are three policemen going to deal with two murders in less than forty-eight hours?"

Hammond walked from behind the quilting tent, a notebook in his hand, and strolled over to a small crowd gathered at the next tent.

"Are they going to question everyone?" Holly asked. "Hammond moves at the speed of molasses."

"Gilroy and Underhill just joined in," I said, tossing my head in the direction of the tent. "How's Peter doing?"

"He's fine. Not thrilled by the cleanup, but we're both glad it wasn't worse." She angled herself on the bench to face me. "How do you think the break-in is connected to the murders?"

"It has the look of someone trying to scare you off. On the morning you found the note on your front door, how many people did you talk to about it?"

"Oh, a lot. I wasn't very subtle, but at the time I didn't think it was anything more than a nasty prank."

"Is Tom Ventura on the Board of Trustees?" I asked.

"Where did that come from?"

I lifted a shoulder. "Just wondering. I should know these things." I thought hard about telling her that Ventura had implied he would no longer be a supporter of her bakery, whatever that meant for her future business, but she had enough on her plate.

"He and five others, yes. Then there's the mayor, and that's our entire town government."

"Here comes Chief Gilroy," Julia said. She squirmed in her seat just a little, and I had to squelch a grin.

"Ladies, thanks for waiting," Gilroy said. He got right to it. "Can you tell me where you were when . . . ?" His meaning obvious, he let his words trail off.

"When we heard the scream?" I asked. A gentle jab, but I should have kept my mouth shut. It occurred to me that I was trying to get the stony-faced Gilroy to react. *Wanted* him to react. The idea horrified me.

"We were all in the coffee tent," Julia said, pointing to her left. "Over there, waiting for the rain to stop. When it did, we came outside the tent but kind of hovered around." She made circles in the air with her hands. "I think Rachel saw her first."

Time to act like an adult. "She was walking around the tent, holding on to it as if she might pass out," I said.

"Then she screamed. I ran over there at about the same time everyone else did. I didn't see anything out of the ordinary, except . . ." I hesitated before continuing. "Just before the rain started and everyone ran inside the tents, Tom Ventura looked startled by something. Or someone."

"Startled," Gilroy said flatly.

I revised my statement. "Shocked."

"But you don't know by what."

"Maybe he saw Aiden."

"Why would that shock him?"

"Maybe Aiden wasn't supposed to be here." I told Gilroy about seeing Aiden and Ventura at the Lilac Lane B&B, and for good measure I told him I'd seen Newsome there too. "Ventura and Aiden were buddies, Newsome and Aiden were buddies, and for all I know, all three of them were buddies. They were up to something, starting with those notes. And Ventura and Newsome are still up to something."

Realizing that Gilroy was glaring at me, I stopped talking.

"Do you normally hang around the Lilac Lane?" he asked.

"It's my home away from home."

Holly jabbed me with her elbow.

"Here's my card," he said, reaching into his shirt pocket. "Call me if any of you remember anything."

"You gave me your card day before yesterday," I said.

Julia snatched the card from his hands. "Is there any progress on my husband's murder?"

"We're still working on it. I'll let you know if there is."

"It has to be connected to Aiden's murder."

"It might be," Gilroy said, rubbing his eyes.

For once the chief's brief replies seemed more the product of exhaustion than his brusque nature.

"And ladies," he said, "there have been two murders now. For your own safety, please don't meddle."

Meddle. The nerve. After I'd handed him several pertinent pieces of information, starting yesterday with the fact that Aiden Dillard was the mysterious note writer.

Gilroy sauntered off, and when he was out of earshot, I said, "You two meet me in twenty minutes at my house. I'll make coffee and order lunch." I stood and marched straight for the parking area of the field.

It wasn't until the three of us were settled into couches in my living room, coffees in hand after we'd devoured two pineapple and pepperoni pizzas, that I told Julia and Holly I may have seen something important at the festival. "Trouble is, everyone moved about so much it was hard to keep track of them. Maybe I didn't see anything. Maybe I just had the feeling that something bad was about to happen."

"I was watching you from the coffee tent," Julia said, "and I lost sight of you and Aiden right away."

"But I think they were moving in relation to one another," I said, the image of a chess board still fresh in my mind. "Reacting to how the others were moving. Watching one another."

Setting her cup on my pine end table, Holly lifted herself from the couch and tucked one leg beneath her. "Who is 'they'?"

I dashed into the kitchen, returned with a yellow

notepad and pen, and dropped back into my armchair. "Aiden, Newsome, and Ventura," I said, jotting their names. "Newsome and Ventura both knew Aiden and they both knew he was in town. All three of them were there. So was Douglas McDermott."

"Don't forget Gilroy and Hammond," Holly said. "They both lived in Juniper Grove seven years ago, and they're not above suspicion."

Julia protested. "Gilroy and Hammond? Those two couldn't murder anyone."

"Holly's right," I said. "We can't rule out anyone." Without thinking, I added, "Belinda Almond was there too."

Julia grunted.

It was time to fess up. "I met her yesterday, Julia. I think the *Post* treated her unfairly."

Julia cocked an eyebrow. She wasn't speaking, just staring—a bad sign.

"Belinda insists she didn't have an affair with your husband. She says the *Post*'s photographer snapped a photo at a party at just the wrong time, trying very hard to leave that impression." I didn't mention that George had instigated the situation that resulted in the dubious photograph.

"And you believe her?" Julia asked, her eyes filled with reproach.

Tread carefully, I thought. *Julia has lived the truth of this affair for more than seven years*. "Isn't it possible that Jillian Newsome made Belinda look guilty the same way she made you look guilty?"

Holly perked up.

"The way she made me look and sound evasive?" I

added. "I have nothing to do with this, but she made it look like I did—and without breaking libel laws." I leaned forward. "She did the same thing to Chief Gilroy, making it sound as though he left Fort Collins under a cloud of scandal."

Julia was tugging at her earlobe, considering my words.

"Even Tom Ventura dislikes her." I flipped open the pizza boxes in the vain hope I'd find leftovers, but only a few globs of cheese remained.

"Belinda never said a word in her own defense to me," Julia said.

"How could she, especially after your husband disappeared? I think she's heartbroken that people believe the rumors."

"But George didn't deny the rumors," Julia said, finally letting go of her ear.

"Julia," Holly said, her voice kind but firm, "George Foster was not a good man, and more than once I saw him flirt with women at parties."

"You did? You never said."

"I couldn't. But believe me, the interest was *never* returned."

A serial flirter who probably relished rumors of his prowess. I had figured there was a pattern to Foster's behavior. No wonder he hadn't denied the affair with Belinda, even to his wife. "Is that party photo of Belinda the only proof of their affair?" I asked.

Julia swallowed hard. "Rachel, have I been wrong all this time? I knew George liked to pretend he was irresistible to women. He was always pretending."

"I've only lived here a few months, but I know you

wouldn't be the first person Newsome has fooled. She's good at what she does."

"I haven't treated Belinda very well," Holly said. "I'm polite but cool. What if we've both been wrong?"

"And what if I've been wrong about Chief Gilroy?" I said. "I treat him like a bumpkin, but I don't think he is."

"The *Post* likes to portray him that way," Holly said.

"I wonder why." My eyes shifted to Julia. "So I've been fooled too. All we can do is start fresh."

"I need to talk to Belinda," Julia said. "If I think she's telling the truth about George, I'll have to ask her forgiveness."

"Meanwhile," I said, giving my notepad a pat, "she's still on the suspect list for Aiden's murder until we can rule her out."

"Though if Belinda was going to kill anyone, you'd think it would be Newsome," Holly said. She held up a hand. "Not that I wish murder on her."

"Speak for yourself," Julia said, her lips slanting into a smile.

"Peter dislikes her more than I do. He wants to cancel our subscription."

"Peter's a wise and fine man," Julia said.

"I was lucky to find him," Holly said, her tone suddenly serious. "Rachel, can I ask you something? Why haven't you married?"

The question took me by surprise. I'd heard it before from other people, and I'd always evaded it one way or another. "You know, well, time passes, and then, you know, before you know it . . . ," I said, fumbling for words and doing a particularly poor job of it.

"There must have been someone once," Julia said.

I nodded. "Twelve years ago."

Her interest piqued, Julia sat straighter. Which oddly made me all the more reluctant to talk. But I was among friends, and friends opened up to one another—as Julia had about George.

"We were engaged," I said. My gaze strayed to the window overlooking my front garden, where my pink and white roses still glistened with rain. "And then he left and moved to Arizona."

"You mean before you were married?" Holly asked.

"Yup." I looked back at my friends, at their expressions of surprise and pity, and wanted to drop the matter right then. Julia wouldn't let me.

"Did he give you a reason?" she asked.

"No, he just left, a week before the wedding. I found out from one of his friends."

Holly's lip curled in disgust. "What a rotten, stinking thing to do. Oh, Rachel, I'm so sorry."

I shrugged. "It was twelve years ago."

"You still love him," Julia declared. "But you shouldn't think about him, just like I shouldn't think about George. You have to move on."

"He was the love of my life," I said, forcing a smile. "A wonderful man who asked me to marry him and then didn't even have the courage to tell me the wedding was off. I was still young back then, you know?"

Neither Julia nor Holly spoke. I'd said enough—more than enough. Giving my knees a slap, I rose from my armchair and brandished the yellow notepad. "We've got work to do. Who murdered Julia's husband and how is that snake in the grass Newsome involved? More coffee anyone?"

CHAPTER 11

Julia and I played cards on most Saturday nights. It had become an enjoyable ritual, though Julia sometimes observed that it was strange I'd prefer playing Rummy 500 to going out. But after too much pizza, just enough coffee, and three hours of discussing George Foster's and Aiden Dillard's murders, Julia, Holly, and I called it a day. In the morning we would study the case with fresh eyes.

I decided the best course of action was to work on my writing—I'd been thrown off schedule by a couple days—and then make an early night of it. That was the plan, that is, until I heard a rap at my front door and found Belinda Almond on my doorstep.

"I'm sorry to bother you so late," she said.

"It's no bother, come in," I replied, waving her inside. "And it's not that late."

"It was dark, so I didn't know if you were in."

I flicked on the living room and then the kitchen lights. "I was writing upstairs. Keeps the electric bills down. Can I get you something to drink?"

"No, thanks."

I motioned for her to sit at the table and then started

the coffeemaker. "Decaf," I explained.

Belinda slung her jacket on the back of a chair and took a seat. "You have a beautiful kitchen."

"Thank you." It was nice, and serviceable, with honey-colored cabinets and not-too-shabby faux-granite countertops, but no one had ever called my kitchen beautiful. "So what can I do for you?"

"You know about Aiden Dillard, of course."

"I was at the festival. I saw you briefly but never got the chance to talk to you."

"I saw you too, after they found the body—after I saw it. I can't get it out of my mind." She kept her hands busy, fingering nicks on the tabletop, playing with her earring.

"Have you heard anything? Do you know whose knitting needle that was?"

Belinda shivered. "No, I haven't heard a word. I'm sure something will be in the paper tomorrow, whether or not it's true. I hate the idea of having to buy that birdcage liner so I can find out the news, and probably not the real news, at that. Good thing I don't have to buy it very often."

I poured myself a cup of decaf, sat, and cleared my throat, hoping Belinda would take it as a signal to broach her subject. Something was worrying her, but she seemed to want to distract herself from it, to postpone saying what she had come to say.

She took a breath, gathering strength. "I overheard something at the festival. I was in the quilting tent, near the back flap, and I heard Tom Ventura and Chase Hammond talking outside the tent, only a foot or two away from me. There was a lot of noise inside the tent, but you see"—she spread her hands—"I was closer to them than I was to the sellers inside. I saw their shadows on the tent."

"I take it their conversation was out of the ordinary."

"After two murders, I'd normally go to the police if I heard something like that, only Hammond *is* the police, and Ventura's an attorney. You're the only person I can trust."

"Why me?"

"Because you're new to town. You don't have a stake or a history in any of this."

I saw her point. "Tell me exactly what they said."

"They were talking about Chief Gilroy and Jillian Newsome. Ventura said, 'I can't believe Newsome is double . . .'" Her eyes shut briefly as she tried to recall his words. "'Double-dealing me,' that's it. He said he told her to stay away from Aiden Dillard and just keep reporting on Gilroy, and now he was afraid things were about to get out of control."

"This was before Aiden was killed?"

"Before."

"Go on."

"Then Officer Hammond said he was tired of waiting for his time to come, that Newsome was complicating things, and that Ventura should never have brought Gilroy in from Fort Collins. After that someone must have walked by, because they stopped talking and split up."

"Tired of waiting for his time to come," I repeated, recalling my first meeting with Gilroy and Hammond at my house. "When I asked Gilroy and Hammond if they were living in Juniper Grove at the time of the Foster-Dillard disappearance, Gilroy said he'd just become chief, and Hammond said he was an officer back then, just like he is now."

"That's true."

"But it was the way Hammond said it. *Just like I am*

now, with a touch of bitterness."

"Like he hadn't advanced in seven years."

"And Gilroy gave him a look I couldn't quite figure out then, but it makes sense now."

"That doesn't explain what Ventura meant by Newsome double-dealing him."

"Did Ventura or Hammond sound like they were making threats against Newsome or Aiden Dillard?"

"To be honest, no." Belinda sounded a little disappointed. What she'd heard was evidence of collusion between a police officer and town attorney, but what kind of collusion wasn't clear. "And they didn't say a word about George Foster."

"But they're up to no good, and Gilroy's at the bad end of it." Warning Gilroy was out of the question, at least for now. He'd told me to stop meddling, and though I had no intention of backing off, I wasn't going to draw undue attention to my investigation.

How quickly I'd gone from having to be dragged into what I was now calling "the case" to stubbornly insisting I was going to see it through until the end. Yes, I wanted to help Julia, but I also wanted to see justice for her—and justice meant finding out what Newsome was up to. Or as it now appeared, Newsome, Ventura, and Hammond working together. They had tormented Julia and Belinda, and it seemed they were out to ruin Chief Gilroy. Newsome would make sure derogatory articles were published, and Ventura and Hammond would . . . do what? "I wonder why Officer Hammond said Newsome was complicating things."

"She was sticking her nose in?" Belinda suggested. "That's what she does best."

My coffee was getting cold, but I was no longer interested. I pushed the cup to the middle of the table and leaned back in my chair. "Let's say Newsome was supposed to make Gilroy look bad in the *Post*. That was her job. But she found out Aiden Dillard was in town and started meeting with him. I saw Newsome with Aiden and Ventura with Aiden, but I've never seen the three together." I lifted my shoulders in a shrug. "Just a wild guess."

"Do you think one of them is a murderer?"

"Aiden might have become a problem by becoming so visible," I said, "but why would any of them kill George Foster?" But murderers or not, Newsome, Ventura, and Hammond were dangerous people, willing to use the power of their offices to destroy lives. "Don't talk to anyone about this," I added. "Gilroy, maybe, but no one else."

"I think the chief needs to know that Hammond is out to get his job."

"The way he looked at Hammond in my house, he already knows." A new thought came to mind. "Did you see Mayor McDermott at the festival?"

"I expected to, since he's the mayor, but no."

"He was there, poor man." I told her about McDermott's dash from the coffee tent, in what was probably a futile attempt to escape Newsome.

"Thanks for that," Belinda said. "It's something happy to think about on my way home." She stood, slipped her arms into her jacket, and started for the door. "And thanks for listening to me."

"Belinda," I said, resting my hand on the doorknob, "I know McDermott wasn't mayor seven years ago, but was he in politics?"

"He was on the Board of Trustees for a while, back when they hired Chief Gilroy."

"He quit?"

"He and Ventura got into some public fights during board meetings. Not horrendous, but they didn't like each other. I always thought Ventura didn't care, but McDermott did. He didn't like the conflict."

Being mayor was not exactly a conflict-free career, I thought. "Is McDermott Ventura's boss?"

"The town attorney is hired by the board and the mayor, so no, technically. But if McDermott wanted to, he could ask the board to dismiss Ventura, and since the board likes McDermott more than Ventura, in a sense Ventura's job is in the mayor's hands."

As Belinda headed down the front steps for her blue minivan, I wondered if Julia had seen her arrive. It was too late at night, I hoped, Julia being more of a morning and afternoon window sentry. I would tell her about Belinda's visit, but in my own time.

I watched Belinda pull from the curb, heading east on Finch Hill Road. Two second later, a dark-colored SUV did the same.

I darted out of the house and down my front steps, hoping whoever was in the SUV would see me—and know I'd seen them following Belinda—but the SUV's taillights dissolved into the night. Though I told myself I was imagining danger where there was none, I'd never seen that SUV before, and on my quiet street at this time of night, two vehicles leaving the curb and heading east at the same time amounted to an impossibility. I grabbed my car keys and phone and shot out my back door for the garage.

In record time, I was driving east, searching the road

for Belinda's minivan. At Bayberry Street, I saw a dark SUV ahead of me, but no sign of Belinda's minivan. I followed onto Lookout Road and was soon on the outskirts of town. The SUV's headlights illuminated the road in front of it, but not the black, empty spaces beyond. I was driving down a darkened corridor, with no idea where I was going and who was leading me. "Where are you, Belinda?" I said aloud.

Pressing softly on the brake, I slowed the Forester, but rather than pull away from me, the SUV matched my new speed. The driver was watching. Woman or man? I squinted, but the tint on the back window obscured even the shape of the driver.

With a growing sense of fear, I strained to catch a number or letter on the license plate. I dropped farther back, letting my headlights' beam shine over plate. "MO . . ."

The SUV screeched to a stop and I hit my brakes.

I saw the headlights go dark. "This is not good."

The driver's door popped open, but no one inside the SUV moved.

I realized then that I had the upper hand. If the driver wanted to threaten me, he or she would have to exit the car—right into my headlights. I'd know who it was, and I'd know it from the safety of my car. Keeping my eyes on the SUV, I picked up my phone and snapped a photo of the license plate.

The driver's door slammed shut and the SUV took off.

"Gotcha," I said.

CHAPTER 12

Being a newcomer to town had its advantages. Belinda saw my outsider status as reason to trust me. But as a newcomer, I was beginning to see suspects everywhere. Julia and Holly were trustworthy, but that was as far as I was willing to go. As I fixed breakfast and looked back on last night's car chase, I began to view even Belinda with distrust. Her minivan had simply disappeared, yet somehow the SUV two seconds behind her had found me—chased me from ahead, in essence.

I'd felt safe and victorious after snapping a photo of the license plate, but with the morning light, the reality of what had happened began to set in. At a minimum, someone had wanted to frighten me. And I'd foolishly offered myself up, hopping into my car and racing into the night without a second thought.

As I got ready for church, I tried unsuccessfully to banish unchurchly things from my mind. If Belinda was there, as she usually was, I needed to ask her what had happened to her last night. Truth is, I didn't know where she lived. She could have taken a turn at any point without me seeing her minivan. Judging her on paltry evidence wasn't fair or smart. Then, after church, I'd ask Julia and

Holly if they knew how to trace a Colorado license plate number on Sunday. On a weekday it was no problem. Pay a fee, get the name associated with the plate. But I wasn't willing to wait until Monday.

By the time Julia was at my front door, I'd decided that Chief Gilroy and Mayor McDermott were equally deserving of my mistrust. What did I, the newbie, know about any of these people? I had my instincts, but instincts were fallible, and I wasn't going to bet my safety on them.

"Holly isn't coming," Julia said, standing just inside the doorway. "Cleanup at the bakery."

Groaning, I threw my head back. "I'd forgotten all about that. She had a crew there yesterday, didn't she?"

"From what I hear. Come on, we're late." Julia tugged at my sleeve until I was out the door.

It didn't escape her notice that I locked both the doorknob and the deadbolt. "I'll tell you later," I said, shoving my keys in my purse. "Now what about the cleaning crew? Do you think we should head over there after church?"

"She's fine and the bakery's clean, but she wants to . . . well, you know Holly," she said with a knowing look.

"Rearrange things."

"The vandalism was an opportunity for her to rethink the front layout before she opens tomorrow."

I laughed. "I'll bet Peter likes that."

"As long as she doesn't change her recipes."

"Heaven forbid."

Julia drove, and I kept an eye out for an SUV bearing the license plate MOY3998. A block from the church, she noticed my unusual interest in dark-colored vehicles, but I held off. "I'll explain after the service."

Inside Trinity Church, Chief Gilroy had taken his usual spot on the second pew back. I couldn't fault him since we all stuck with familiar seats. Julia, Holly, Peter, and I always sat two pews behind him. And Officer Hammond was in his spot in the next section over, with his wife and two young children. Was his family why Hammond was willing to stab Gilroy in the back? I wondered. After all, Gilroy didn't have a wife or children, so it must have seemed doubly unfair to Hammond that Gilroy advanced and he didn't.

Belinda Almond sat directly behind Hammond, and Jillian Newsome, to my surprise, sat two pews behind Belinda. Newsome hadn't been in church since Christmas, so my radar went off. She was here for a purpose.

My radar was verified when Newsome swiveled her head and zeroed in on me. She held up her hands, as if on a steering wheel, wiggled them, and grinned. So much for needing to trace that license plate.

Julia nudged me, but I continued to stare at Newsome. Reasoning that I would eventually find out it had been her on that dark road, she'd decided to spook me. But why? For a lark? Still, knowing it had been her in that SUV made me feel less anxious. I could hold my own against that woman. Still grinning, Newsome gave me a little wave of her hand.

I looked away. This was not the time or place.

After the service, I promptly led Julia to her car in the parking lot. It was more to keep from saying the uncharitable words I was thinking than to simply avoid a confrontation with Newsome. I didn't trust my mouth. And I knew that in my anger, I might reveal everything I knew about what she'd been up to.

Standing on the passenger side of Julia's car, leaning on the door frame, I watched Newsome leave church alone, without speaking to anyone. A few seconds later Belinda left too, also alone. Had Belinda set me up last night?

"Rachel, if you're not getting in the car," Julia called out, "why did you drag me out here like a house on fire?"

"Sorry," I said, getting in and buckling up. "There's something I wanted to tell you."

"There's something I've been wanting to tell you, too." She put her key in the ignition but didn't start it.

"You first," I said.

She drew herself up, straightening her spine. "There won't be a funeral for George. I've decided." Her voice was firm and unemotional. She would not be moved from her resolve. "It would be a circus. I'm having a cremation, and I'll spread his ashes privately."

"I think that's sensible, though I'm sorry it has to be this way."

"I'm not."

I looked her square in the eye. She meant it.

"George and I drifted apart long before he deserted me," she said. "Finding him dead was shocking, but when I saw him, I felt more anger than anything else. Does that make sense?"

"It's exactly how I would feel."

"If you saw the man who deserted you twelve years ago?"

"Let's not get into that."

"What was his name?"

"Brent." I pointed at her keys. "Start the car."

"What were you going to tell me?"

"I'll tell you later," I said. My mind had drifted elsewhere and was now grappling with a question I should have asked myself the night I found George Foster in my backyard. "Julia, where do you think George was for seven years? He couldn't have been in Juniper Grove, and probably not in Colorado. Did they stop looking for him after Dillard's body was found?"

"After about two weeks. I think the Juniper Grove Police thought he was dead, but federal officials weren't so sure."

"That means George had to be very careful. And be careful spending that money."

"The bills weren't marked, and the serial numbers weren't recorded. All he had to do was not spend it right away and not spend a lot at one time."

"When Mitch Dillard was killed on the river, George ended up with all that money to himself."

Julia sighed and leaned back on the headrest. "Do you think what people say is true? That George buried money in your yard? He could have buried part of it, and when he ran out of money, he came back to Juniper Grove."

I shook my head. "I think it's like Gilroy said. There was no time to bury any part of the money. They were on the run. George returned to dig up something else. Question is, who knew he was back in town?" The only answer that made sense to me was Aiden Dillard. Somehow Aiden had found out and spread the word. Did he contact Newsome first? Maybe. And then, possibly, Ventura. But the order didn't matter to Ventura, who complained that Aiden had been double-dealing him by talking to Newsome. Ventura wanted to use the power of the press to remove Gilroy from office, period, and Aiden had made a jumble of his perfectly simple plan.

"Home?" Julia said, starting the car.

"Let's go see Holly. I found something out last night."

We drove downtown, miraculously found a parking place right in front of Holly's Sweets, and got out. Remembering yesterday, and my unfortunate and literal run-in with Belinda, I glanced across the street at the newspaper box. "Julia, did you get the paper this morning?"

"I'll show it to you later."

Her reply made me nervous.

"You're not in it for once," she added.

Paying no attention to the Closed sign on the front door, Julia knocked loudly. A minute later, Holly let us in. The bakery's warm air carried the aromas of sugar, chocolate, and fruit fillings. For the next few minutes, with great restraint, I ignored my rumbling tummy and told them both about my conversation with Belinda and my foolish race to warn her about the dark SUV on her tail.

"Turns out it was Jillian Newsome behind the wheel," I finished. "She let me know in church today."

"Whoa," Holly said. She wandered to one of the small tables against the wall and sat, Julia and me joining her. "There's a lot going on, isn't there? Not just murder, but this—"

"Corruption," I said. "Corruption and collusion."

"Poor Chief Gilroy," Julia said.

"Now all the stories in the paper about his incompetence make sense," I admitted. "Newsome, Hammond, and Ventura want him out, and they were using Aiden." I reconsidered. "Or Aiden was using them."

"He never stopped by after the break-in," Holly said. She was obviously miffed by what she saw as Gilroy's apathetic attitude.

"He's trying to solve two murders," Julia said.

"But I think the break-in is connected to the murders," Holly said.

"So do I," I said, "but indirectly."

"Hang on, we need fuel for our brains." Holly dashed into the back of the bakery and returned with napkins and a plate of muffins. She set the plate ceremoniously in the center of the table. "Chocolate and coffee flavored muffins with a toffee crunch-crumble top."

"Good grief," I said appreciatively. "How did you find the time to do this?"

"I had better find the time—I'm opening tomorrow morning at ten o'clock."

"Good for you!" Julia said.

We enthusiastically dug in. I took large bites from the crumbly muffin top—the best part—while Julia and Holly, the more delicate eaters, tore bite-sized pieces from their muffins and plunked them in their mouths.

"I have a question," Holly said, a bite of muffin halfway to her lips. "Ventura recommended Gilroy's hiring, so why does he want him gone?"

"I can't figure that out," I said, chewing between sentences. "Except Ventura may be as ambitious as Hammond. Hammond becomes police chief and Ventura becomes mayor with Hammond's help."

Julia cleared her throat. "Speaking of."

Holly and I turned toward the bakery door, where Chief Gilroy stood, his fist poised to knock.

"It's about time," Holly mumbled, heading for the

door.

Gilroy walked up to our table and gave us a nod of his head. He was in his usual uniform—jeans, shirt, suit jacket, no tie—but I sensed he was on the job, even on Sunday. "Ladies, I'm sorry to interrupt you." He stuffed his hands in his pockets. "Mrs. Stowe, have you got a moment? I'd like to speak to you alone."

"It's Miss Stowe," Julia said.

"It's Rachel," I corrected, rising from table.

Once we were outside on the sidewalk, Gilroy turned to me and said, "I don't want to worry you, but your name has come up in several of my interviews, and not in a good way."

"Oh, really?" *How nice of you to say.*

"I'm concerned about your safety. There's more going on here than you know."

"I'm more aware than you think I am." He did have the most piercing blue eyes I'd ever seen, and I wondered idly if he knew that, or knew how hard it was to talk to him like an adult while looking into those eyes. "Let me guess. You're talking about Jillian Newsome and Tom Ventura."

Nothing. Not a word, not a flinch.

I pressed on. "Or do you mean Officer Hammond?"

That got a flinch.

"Chief Gilroy, it's not me who should be worried." I made up my mind on the spot. He was warning me, and I was determined to return the favor, come what may. "Those three are working together to get you fired."

Rather than ask me how I knew that, he glared and said, "Rachel, what have you gotten into?"

"I'm trying to help."

"I don't need your help. I'm more aware than you

think I am."

He was silent and solitary so much of the time that I had no idea what he knew or didn't know. He never let on. But underestimating him had become a habit with me. "I sure hope you are." The words sounded harsher than I'd intended. It sounded as though I was challenging his skill and intelligence. *I hope you're smarter than you look.*

"Two people have died." He paused, letting that sink in. "Do you understand that?"

Now he was calling *me* stupid. "And my friend has had her life turned upside down by that beast of a newspaper editor, who no one ever challenges. Now I'm saying she's after you. You're welcome." I spun on my heels and marched back into the bakery, leaving Gilroy on the sidewalk. Certain my words had righteously hit their mark, I turned to see the expression on his face, but all I saw was the back of him as he crossed the street.

CHAPTER 13

Back home in my kitchen, eating a microwaved slab of lasagna I'd found in the freezer, I was alternately sorry and angry about my talk with Chief Gilroy. I'd been rude, no sense denying it, but he'd been condescending. Though condescension was practically a job requirement for police chiefs. Still, I'd challenged his authority and blurted out what I knew about Ventura, Newsome, and Hammond. Had I done that to warn him or to show him how sharp I was? A little of both. Monday morning I'd seek him out and clear the air.

I took my empty plate to the sink, going over George Foster's death in my mind. Because on one point I wouldn't give in to Gilroy: I would not put an end to my investigation. I wandered to my living room window and looked out over my garden. How lucky I'd been to find a house with an established garden full of roses and peonies—and in the early spring, grape hyacinths and pasqueflowers. The house itself, in a mild state of disrepair when I'd bought it, was a work in progress, but it was cozy enough, and I had all the time in the world to restore it. The plan had been to write a few hours and then work on the house a few hours, six days a week, making just enough money from my books to get by. Investigating real-life murders hadn't been part of the plan, but I was hooked on the excitement of it.

Where had George Foster been for seven years? Why did he come back? And why did his return incite murder? It was no coincidence that Foster showed up in Juniper Grove three days after a court officially declared him dead, and no coincidence that Aiden Dillard showed up at the same time. Or that the plot to have Chief Gilroy removed from office went into high gear on both men's return.

Looking out the window, pondering the few clear facts at my disposal, I saw a Juniper Grove Police SUV pull up to Julia's house and Officer Hammond get out. As Holly had pointed out, Hammond moved at the speed of molasses. So what was so important he had to visit Julia on a Sunday?

I hurried back into the kitchen, grabbed the extra muffin I'd bought at the bakery, stuck it on a plate, and dashed out the front door. It was the perfect excuse—a muffin for her breakfast tomorrow. Okay, maybe not so perfect, but it was all I had, and I wanted to hear what the slippery Officer Hammond had to say. If what he had to say was about George, I needed to be there for Julia.

Julia was glad to see me, yanking me inside by the arm, telling me that Hammond had stopped by with the autopsy report on George.

A flicker of annoyance crossed Hammond's face as he glanced down at the muffin. "Like I was saying, we got the autopsy back yesterday, but with the trouble at the festival, it got pushed to the back burner. Would you like to go someplace private?" He jabbed a thumb in the direction of the kitchen.

"No, I want Rachel to stay." Julia took the plate from my hands, thanked me, and pivoted back to Hammond. "I'm sorry Officer Hammond, what were you saying?"

"Cause of death was what it first appeared to be—two blows to the head with the shovel blade. The medical examiner said he would have lost consciousness almost instantly on the first blow, and death would have followed in a matter of minutes. Your husband didn't suffer."

"I see." Visibly relieved, Julia set the plate on a lamp table. "I did wonder how long he was there, maybe calling for help or in pain."

"The ME is sure that didn't happen," Hammond said. "You don't need to give it another thought."

"Thank you for telling me, and for coming all the way out here."

Hammond smiled. "It's not that far, Mrs. Foster, and I thought you should know."

By all appearances, Hammond was genuinely concerned for Julia and anxious to put her mind at ease. Was it possible to be wildly ambitious to the point you'd betray your boss but still have a softer side?

"Then the murderer was a man?" I said tentatively. If so, that would leave out Newsome, though killing a young, healthy man with a knitting needle also took a certain measure of strength. Or stealth. "Would a woman be able to kill with two blows like that?"

"In my experience, almost any adult could do it," Hammond said. "Especially since he was hit by the edge of the blade, not the flat part." His eyes shot to Julia's. "Sorry, Mrs. Foster."

"I'm just fine. Remember, I'm the one who found

him," Julia said.

I hurried to change the subject. "Any news on Aiden Dillard?"

"Won't be until later this week, though I don't think the cause of death is in doubt."

Hammond seemed in a chattier mood than when I'd first arrived, so I prodded him for information. "Whose knitting needle was that?"

"Turns out it belonged to one of the ladies of the Juniper Grove Knitting Circle. They were selling knit stuff—scarves and things—and giving knitting demonstrations in one of the tents."

"Someone outside the group must have taken it without them knowing."

"Well, I can't picture eighty-year-old Ida Rudman stabbing a man in the neck."

"Are there any suspects?"

Hammond tilted his head to one side. "You know I can't tell you that."

"Everyone at the festival is a suspect, isn't that right, Officer?" Julia said, sidestepping Hammond, scurrying for the door, and swinging it wide. "Thank you again for stopping by. It was so kind of you. Don't let us keep you."

Hammond hesitated. "If you have any questions—"

"Would you like the muffin?" Julia said.

"The what?"

Julia pointed. "The muffin on the plate over there. You're welcome to it. It's the least I can offer, and I can get a new one tomorrow."

"Um . . ." Hammond moved for the door. "Um, no, you keep it, Mrs. Foster. I'm due home for dinner."

Julia flashed a treacly smile. "Bye, now." She shut the

door and leaned against it, still smiling. “At my age you can get rid of anyone by acting a little ditzy. People so readily believe you are.”

I laughed. My friend was as far from a ditz as anyone I’d ever known, younger or older. “What are you up to?”

Julia whisked the muffin plate from the table and gestured for me to follow her into the kitchen. “I didn’t want to talk about autopsies anymore.”

“It’s more than that.”

“Sit down.”

I obediently sat, and I kept quiet as Julia ran a fork through the muffin and handed me half.

“You don’t mind sharing, do you?” she asked.

“That’s why I brought it.”

“You brought it to snoop on Officer Hammond.”

“What he said caused you to remember something, right?”

Julia dropped her fork to the plate. “That’s not fair. How do you know?”

“It’s obvious. You have something to tell me, but you didn’t call or come over. Hammond arrives, talks, and you suddenly need to get rid of him. You don’t want him to know what he said that struck a chord with you because he’s disloyal to Gilroy. So you’ll tell me and Holly first and then Gilroy.”

“Show-off.”

Crossing my arms on the table, I leaned forward. “But I have no idea what he said, and you do.”

Julia’s eyes were lit with excitement. “I saw something at the festival. When I got there, I started looking for you and Holly. I went first to the coffee tent, but you weren’t there. Then I thought, I know, I’ll try the other tents. And one of them was the knitting and crochet tent."

"This is getting interesting."

"And guess who was in there. Mayor McDermott and Jillian Newsome. Together, I mean, and talking in a corner of the tent as if they didn't want anyone to overhear them."

"Funny how everyone says they dislike Newsome but they always end up chatting with her."

"They weren't arguing, that's for sure."

"McDermott told me he hopes Newsome leaves Juniper Grove for a bigger market."

"It didn't look like he was hoping any such thing."

"Then again, he's the mayor. He can't ignore people like Newsome if she wants to talk to him."

Julia put a hand on my forearm, silencing me. "That's not all. When the mayor left the tent, Jillian stayed behind, and she was staring—Rachel, I mean staring—at the knitting needles." She flopped back in her chair, pleased with herself for having recalled the incident. "I didn't think anything of it at the time because she's such a strange woman, but when Officer Hammond said the needle that killed Aiden was from the knitting circle, I realized what I'd seen."

"Did she touch any of the needles?"

Julia frowned and pursed her lips. "I left the tent right after that."

"How long was this before Aiden was found?"

"Ten minutes at most."

I thought hard, trying to remember precisely where everyone had been ten minutes before Aiden was killed.

"So?" Julia said impatiently. "That woman has no interest in knitting. Do you think she murdered Aiden?"

"I think it's significant that she was staring at the needles, and you have to tell Gilroy."

"Significant how?" Julia popped a bit of muffin in her mouth.

"It doesn't mean *she* killed Aiden, but you have to ask why she was staring at the needles. I don't believe in coincidences. Did she look at the needles and suddenly see an opportunity? Did she tell someone else and they carried out the murder? A lot of people in Juniper Grove are relieved that Aiden Dillard is out of the way, but I'm not sure Newsome is one of them. Then again, she thrives on bad news and wouldn't mind another murder in town, and Aiden may have become a risky loose end. So if she knew someone wanted to kill Aiden—"

"She wouldn't do anything to stop it."

"She might even help." I stood, my thoughts tumbling. I needed to be alone to think things through, to untangle what had become a spider's web of clues.

"I'm going to the police station tomorrow to tell—"

Julia broke off midsentence as the kitchen phone rang. I was about to make my exit when she mouthed, "It's Holly." She listened intently, shaking her head now and then, and just before hanging up said, "I'll tell her."

"Is Holly still at the bakery?" I asked.

"Yes, and Officer Underhill paid her and Peter an unexpected visit." Julia waved her hands about, unable to contain her excitement. "You'll never guess. The police arrested someone for the vandalism."

"You're joking."

"They found prints, and one of the other store owners said he saw this person lingering around the back entrance." Julia paused, savoring the moment. "It was

Jacob Ventura, Tom Ventura's grandson."

CHAPTER 14

Julia knocked on my front door the next morning, brandishing her special Monday edition of the *Juniper Grove Post*. A photo of Jacob Ventura—copied from the Juniper Grove High yearbook, by the looks of it—was on the front page. "Above the fold," Julia pointed out as she breezed through the door and headed for the kitchen.

"I thought Newsome and Tom Ventura were allies," I said, trailing after her. "Coffee?"

"Please." She tossed the paper on the table and sat. "The article is very critical of Tom and his grandson."

"Our town attorney must be steaming." I started the coffee, joined Julia, and gave the article a quick read. Written by someone other than Newsome for once, it was every bit as cutting as Julia had said, though the writer had at least contacted Tom Ventura for a comment. On arrest, Jacob had immediately confessed to the vandalism. Why he'd broken into the bakery, he wouldn't say. "Ventura is quoted as saying he's very disappointed in his grandson."

"As he should be."

"But nowhere does it suggest why Jacob chose Holly's Sweets as a target."

"And you don't believe in coincidences."

"I do not. Why was he silly enough to leave prints?"

"He's a teenager."

I poured Julia and myself a cup of coffee, and while she drank and gazed out my back window, and talked about the warm days of summer coming to an end, I flipped through the paper, scanning it for other articles of interest. There were two lengthy articles on Aiden Dillard's murder, a single article on the George Foster murder, and three letters to the editor calling Chief James Gilroy an amateur and a disgrace to Juniper Grove. Yet Gilroy was the one who had quickly found and arrested Jacob Ventura.

"I wonder if Newsome is soliciting these anti-Gilroy letters," I said.

"She's probably writing them herself," Julia said, setting down her cup. "I've never heard of those letter writers. Made-up names, if you ask me."

"At the same time, she's going pretty hard on Tom Ventura's grandson."

"All she really cares about is shocking news and paper sales, so she got what she wanted."

"And she's helping Ventura and Hammond get what they want. Hammond as police chief and Ventura as mayor." I sipped at my coffee, checking for the temperature, then gulped it down. "Though I wonder if his grandson getting arrested will put a crimp in his political plans."

"Tom Ventura's a good man, and he tried his best but couldn't control his grandson," Julia said sarcastically. "Can't we all identify with that? The poor man. And Jacob—the misguided youth with a heart of gold. Trust me, Rachel, the next article about Jacob will be very sympathetic, especially toward his grandfather. In the end, this will only help Ventura become mayor."

Jillian Newsome cleverly turning lemons into

lemonade for her accomplice. I hadn't considered that. "First stop this morning is the police station so you can tell Gilroy about Newsome and the knitting needles," I said, collecting our cups and putting them in the sink.

Julia brightened.

"I'm sure he'll appreciate the information," I added with a smile. Unlike me, Julia rarely tried to disguise her feelings. There was a kind of freedom in that, I thought, watching her finger-comb her hair and tug at the hem of her green sweater.

"Ready?" she said, already moving for the back door.

Five minutes later I pulled into a parking space in front of the police station, right next to the chief's SUV. That meant he hadn't left the station yet, unless it was his turn to buy donuts at Holly's Sweets.

Julia and I stepped to the curb, and as I clicked the remote on my key chain, I heard a gruff voice call out Julia's name. I swung toward it. Tom Ventura was bulldozing his way down the sidewalk, the two of us in his sights. My first instinct was to run for the station door, but he looked and sounded so ludicrous that I was frozen in fascination. His glasses perched at the end of his nose, he was gesticulating and shouting, and as he came closer I saw a smear of red jam in the corner of his lips. The man was not happy. Or overly fastidious.

"It's about time," he said, coming to a halt a mere foot from Julia's face.

Julia stood her ground. "Tom Ventura, what on earth are you yelling about? And back up or I'll poke you."

Ventura took half a step back. "You came down here on your own? I told Gilroy to pick you up. You don't get special privileges, I don't care how old you are. There will be no favoritism in my town. If my grandson can be hauled in, then so can you." He stuck out his forefinger, aiming it like a weapon at her face. "No favoritism, do you hear?"

"Calm down," I said. "We have no idea what you're talking about."

Ventura took another half step back, a quizzical expression forming on his face. "Gilroy told you to come in?"

"Unless he has ESP, he doesn't know I'm here," said Julia, now wearing an equally bewildered look. "Stop behaving like a thug and get out of our way."

"Are you saying he didn't tell you to come in?" Ventura's confusion was rapidly turning to anger.

"Why would he?" I asked.

Ventura stared at me, an irate glint in his eye. "Because I told him to."

Drawn by loud voices on the normally peaceful street, a small crowd was gathering on the sidewalk. Julia didn't seem to notice, or care, but I wanted to slink away. "Wait a minute," I began, having trouble believing what I was now thinking. "You asked Chief Gilroy to bring Julia in for questioning?"

He gave a short snort of a laugh. "Not questioning, an arrest."

Julia's hand went to her throat.

"For what?" I asked. "And what gives you the right?"

He thumped his chest. "I'm the town attorney."

"You can't order the police chief to arrest someone." Truthfully, I had no idea what a town attorney could or couldn't do, but I wasn't about to let him bully Julia.

That did it. Ventura did a full pivot my way, like a gun turret on a destroyer. "I have the power to recommend it, and I did. This morning. Wise law enforcement officers listen to town officials. If Gilroy chooses to ignore my informed recommendation, so much the worse for him."

"Tom Ventura, you, you . . . foolish . . ." Julia was puffing and sputtering. "You listen to me. Don't you dare—don't you *dare*—take out your grandson's arrest on me. Your wife and I are friends and you've known me forever. You know I haven't done anything wrong."

Yes, he knows that, I realized, watching a smirk grow wide on his lips. Julia was his pawn. His quarry was Chief Gilroy. "Come on, Julia," I said, pulling her to the station entrance. "Never mind him."

"You had *better* mind me," Ventura said before he stomped off.

A white mug in his hand, Gilroy was exiting his office and heading for the coffeemaker when he saw Julia and me enter the building. It probably didn't escape his notice that Julia, nearly staggering toward him, was still clutching her throat in dismay.

"I've never been arrested in my life," she said, looking up at him.

The chief got it in one second. "You talked to Tom Ventura."

"It was more like he talked to us," I said.

Gilroy set his mug next to the coffeemaker and gave Julia his full attention. "Mrs. Foster, I promise you're not going to be arrested. Don't give it another thought."

"Then why did Tom say that?"

Gilroy considered and responded diplomatically. "He's having a bad week."

It occurred to me that although Ventura's bad week was undeniable, as was his need to ruin Gilroy, as town attorney the man had to present the chief with evidence. He couldn't just get a bug up his nose about someone and ask Gilroy to make an arrest. "Ventura didn't recommend you arrest Julia yesterday, but he did this morning," I said. "What changed? What evidence did he give you?"

"Sorry, I can't talk about that," Gilroy said.

"So he could give this hypothetical evidence to someone else," I said.

Julia sucked in her breath.

Gilroy took a used filter out of the coffeemaker and tossed it in a trash bin. With his back to me, he said, "The town attorney doesn't have anything that any official would call evidence."

I heard it in his voice and saw it in how he turned away from us both—he hated to speak about another official like that, even one he surely disliked, but to ease Julia's mind, he had done it. He was an honorable man surrounded by dishonorable men. Who cared if he had the personality of a stone?

Gilroy's one-sentence reassurance being all Julia needed, she moved on to the real reason for our visit. The chief made notes and thanked her, and a few minutes later, information duly passed along, we were heading for the bakery.

One shop west of the bakery, we encountered Belinda Almond.

Julia had managed to avoid her for years—looking the other way, crossing the street, going down another aisle in the grocery—but there was no dodging this time. Too many things had happened, including the death of Belinda's presumed lover, George.

"Belinda, I've been wanting to talk to you about

Saturday night," I said.

"Oh?"

Both women were taking pains to look past each other, keeping their eyes on me, the sidewalk, or passersby.

"When you left my house, you were followed by Jillian Newsome in her SUV. She was parked outside my house."

"She was? I never saw her."

"I followed you—or I tried to. I ended up following Newsome instead. You didn't see her?"

"To be honest, I wasn't looking. I needed to get home."

"Do you live nearby?"

"On Glen Haven, four blocks south. Why was she parked outside your house?"

"Who knows why that woman does what she does?" Julia said.

My jaw almost dropped. Julia was talking with her great adversary. She must have known in her heart that her husband was a pretend philanderer and Belinda, like many others, was an innocent victim of the *Post*.

"She's terrible, isn't she?" said Belinda, testing the waters.

"That so-called newspaper woman has done more damage to people in this town than anyone or anything else," I said. I speedily amended that. "Except the murderer, of course."

Julia looked from me to Belinda. "They might be one and the same," she said, nodding sagely.

"Really?" Belinda leaned in, giving Julia her due.

Julia proceeded to tell Belinda what she'd seen at the Farmers' Market Festival, and though I wasn't sure it was wise to let on that she'd witnessed the Great Knitting Needle Clue, I thought it worth the risk if it brought the two women together. I hated gossip, but I had to admit it sometimes had that effect on people.

When we parted, Julia and Belinda were acquaintances again. Not friends, but not enemies. Belinda had offered no explanation, Julia had offered no apology. Still, I could imagine a time in the future when Belinda would join Julia, Holly, and me around my kitchen table for coffee, and the thought lifted my spirits.

"Let's say hello to Jillian Newsome," I said, doing an about-face and taking Julia with me.

"What? Why?"

"I'm new in town, and I've never visited the *Juniper Grove Post*."

"She's not going to take you on a tour."

"Just don't mention the knitting needle."

"What are you really up to?"

On the next block west, standing in front of the newspaper's building, I had to admit to Julia that I didn't have a plan, other than to shake a few trees and see what coconuts fell out of them. I'd been too passive in my investigation. What did I care if Newsome wanted to throttle me? On the other hand, Julia didn't need to make more enemies at the *Post*. "You should wait here. I'll be in and out quickly, and you can keep an eye on the street for any of our suspects."

"Suits me fine. After Tom Ventura, I'm not in the mood."

I opened the building's door and entered a long, narrow room full of cubicles. Telephones ringing, voices buzzing, people hopping up from their chairs to hand pieces of paper to other people hopping up from their chairs—it was a level of activity I wouldn't have dreamed possible in a small-town newspaper.

"Excuse me," I said, waylaying a young woman on her way out the door. "Does everyone here work for the *Post*?"

"We do now," she said with a grin. "I've been trying to get a job here for months, and I was hired three days ago. Most of the new people are interns, though."

"Are you all working on—"

"The murders, yes," she said, nodding vigorously.

"Are you investigating—"

"Tips, yes. They're coming in faster than we can handle them."

"On the phone?"

"Or in person." She glanced from side to side. "To tell you the truth, even some cops and politicians are giving us tips. It's insane." She giggled. "That's why they're sending me to Grove Coffee. We need the caffeine."

"Politicians and cops are your sources?"

"I've said too much." She put a finger to her lips. "More than I should have."

"Be careful of these tips," I warned as she started to walk away.

Throwing me an astonished look over her shoulder, she mouthed, "Why?"

The girl was eager and ambitious, two qualities that made her far too willing to trust. *One day you'll find out why*, I thought.

Since no one seemed interested in challenging my authority to walk around the building, I did just that, hunting for Newsome. I found her almost immediately, sitting in a glass-walled office at the end of the narrow room, behind a large desk on which two computer monitors sat, positioned like sentries to her right and left. The *Juniper Grove Post* had become the *Denver Herald.*

I walked toward the office, focusing on the seated figure to the right of her desk, his face obscured by frosted glass. As I drew closer, he stood, revealing himself, and I came to a stop. Officer Hammond plunked his uniform hat on his head and shook Newsome's hand—a hearty, congratulatory shake. The shake of two people working in unison but strictly for their own selfish purposes. Was Hammond also one of the tipsters? Feeding Newsome the kind of information that would help his career path and remove Gilroy from the competition? How I'd misjudged his friendly face.

Hammond reached for the office door. Not wanting him to see me, I started for the exit. Hairs stood on the back of my neck as he neared, his footsteps falling heavy on the floor. "Rachel Stowe?" he called out.

I planted a cheery expression on my face and turned. "Officer Hammond. Why on earth are *you* here?"

He laughed and smiled his open, toothy smile. "Why wouldn't I be?"

"I didn't think the police and the newspaper got along."

"The paper is part of the community."

"The paper thinks it runs the community."

"If you keep on its friendly side, it's not so bad."

"What does keeping it friendly entail, Officer? Helping Jillian Newsome's political agenda?"

His grin vanished. "What?"

"How about leaking details of murder

investigations?" It took every ounce of willpower I possessed to stop short of telling him I knew he was trying to ruin Gilroy.

"Look, you're a writer, and writers like to imagine things," he said. He leaned in close to my face, his breath smelling of coffee and bacon. "For that reason, I'll cut you a break. But don't ever accuse me of being a dirty cop."

CHAPTER 15

I talked Julia into making a stop at the Juniper Grove Library so I could dig up last week's issue of the *Post*. She had tossed her copy after using it to wrap some moldy back-of-the-refrigerator casserole, she told me with glee. Luckily, the library kept print copies of the paper going back two weeks. I needed the issue Julia had brought me Thursday morning, the one on the court's declaration that George Foster was legally dead.

"Why do you have to read this again?" Julia whispered, following me to a large oak table.

I opened the paper on the table, and she leaned in sideways for a better look. "I never read it all," I whispered back. "Remember?"

According to the article, the hearing was perfunctory. Testifying to Foster's presumed death were Chief Gilroy and Officer Hammond, who had found the broken raft and Mitch Dillard's battered body in the rocks of the Blue River. They couldn't imagine Foster surviving the same trip, they told the court. And both testified that as far as they could see, Julia Foster had never benefited financially from her husband's bank theft. As did Tom Ventura, Holly Kavanagh, and Julia's children in Montana and Ohio via written statement. There was no mention of the now-mayor, Douglas McDermott.

"Maybe this is why Holly got one of Aiden's notes," I said under my breath, tapping a finger on the article. "She was vehement in saying George was dead and you never got a penny from him. Everyone who testified in your favor got a note. The police, Ventura, and Holly."

"Yes, of course," Julia said. "Holly wasn't part of the original investigation, but she came to the hearing."

"And Belinda got a note because Aiden believed the newspaper's lies about her and probably thought she'd planned the whole thing with your husband." I leaned back in my chair, puzzling over the twists and turns of the case, how the good guys had turned into bad guys and vice versa. "Tom Ventura did a one-eighty this morning," I said a little too loudly.

Julia cringed and said she was going to "leave me to it" and search for a book on gardening. Her disappearance allowed me to do a search of the microfiche for the paper's photo of Belinda Almond and George Foster at the library benefit party. I wanted to see for myself what the photographer had captured seven-plus years ago. It didn't take long to find the issue that covered the benefit, and from there I simply scrolled down to the third page. There it was.

There was indeed a look of surprise on Belinda's face—and slithery pleasure on Foster's. And yet, in Belinda's eyes I saw something more. If it had been another woman, a woman who hadn't professed her utter distaste for Foster, I might have called it delight. I removed the microfiche sheet and flicked off the machine.

I spotted Julia at the checkout desk, gestured toward the library door, and waited for her to catch up. We walked a block to a small park and sat on a bench under a crabapple tree. Autumn was officially less than a week away, but the day was already warm, and with no storms in the forecast, it would only get warmer. I squinted past the sunlight reflecting off the pond in front of us, out to a thin rectangle of land overgrown with tall grasses and, beyond that, the Lilac Lane B&B's rear parking lot. Questions were running over themselves in my mind, one question overtaking another and then another, like racehorses on a track.

Did Belinda Almond really have an affair with Julia's husband or was I imagining that look in her eyes? More pertinent to my investigation, why did George Foster and Aiden Dillard return to Juniper Grove? Did one know the other was here?

"I always wondered what I would have done if George had left me any of that stolen money," Julia said.

"You would have returned it," I said without hesitation.

"Probably. Not that I had to worry about it."

I sensed a touch of bitterness in her voice. Yes, she would have returned the money, but she'd never had to face the moral quandary because her husband hadn't left her a cent. He hadn't considered her future at all. "I know you, Julia. You wouldn't have kept a penny."

She nodded, resigned to facing the downside of her own principles. "But some people will always believe George left me money. They can't imagine that he wouldn't have."

"Honestly, I can't either. Not even five thousand dollars? The cheapskate."

Julia laughed halfheartedly and said, "He wasn't always that way. Early in our marriage . . ." She fell silent, shaking her head.

My friend put up a good show of having gotten over George's crime, desertion, and double death, but I could see it pained her, and I thought I understood that pain, at least partly. I had planned a life with Brent. He seemed to love me despite my flaws—my too-pointy chin, my thin eyebrows, and the weird cowlick at the back of my head. Yet without even the decency to tell me *why*, he had left. For the longest time I'd felt unworthy. *Felt* being the key word. I understood in my mind that he was the one who had failed and that I was not to blame, but my feelings lagged far behind my thoughts. Brent was not a good man. Then why did I still love him?

I veered away from that thought and redirected my attention to George Foster. He and the bank's vice president had planned the theft, planned the getaway. It all went awry, but surely they had talked it through in detail beforehand. According to Julia, she and George had drifted apart before he left her, but they'd been married for decades, and I couldn't bring myself to believe that meant nothing to a husband, even to a husband like George. "I really can't imagine him not leaving you any money," I said.

"You and me both."

"No, I mean it. I don't believe it." My mind was in a whirl. Was it as simple as that? "It's the timing. I've always wondered about that, but it's obvious, isn't it?"

"The timing of what?"

"Why George came back after seven years." It began to fall together, and suddenly I knew with certainty why George had returned to Juniper Grove. The newspaper article had drawn him. I threw out my hand, gripping

Julia's arm.

"Is this you solving the case?" she said wryly.

"Listen. Maybe your husband didn't have time to bury any money, but he could have asked someone to give you some of it. Either way, somehow, he left you money. And when he saw the article about the court hearing, where you and Holly swore you never saw a cent, he knew it was the truth."

Julia's look of astonishment told me that the thought had never crossed her mind. "I can't think of anyone my George trusted enough to give money to."

"The fact that you've struggled for money these past seven years was the only news in that article that would have drawn George back to Juniper Grove. Everything else was just a retelling of the day he and Dillard stole the money—the same information that's been in the paper a dozen times."

"What about someone at the bank? Could he have given them money?"

"I don't think so. It would be too risky to have three people at the same small bank in on the theft. It had to be someone else. But he returned to Juniper Grove to find out what happened to your money, I'm sure of it. You were supposed to be taken care of, and someone let him down. No, more than that. Someone stole his stolen money." It all made sense, and the more I talked, the more I was convinced. "Aiden Dillard was drawn by the same article. I think the court hearing stirred his resentment over his father's death, and he had to come back, if only to beat the bushes and cause trouble for everyone he blamed. I'll bet he had no idea George was here too."

"One article on one court hearing—"

"Brought them both back."

"And caused their murders," Julia said solemnly. "All because of money."

In the blink of an eye, my logical reconstruction of events came crashing down. "No, wait," I said, slapping my hand to my forehead. "How would they read an article printed in that tiny newspaper? Aiden Dillard was in Utah, and your husband could have been a thousand miles away."

I stood and stretched my back from side to side. I'd been sitting far too much lately, ignoring my trail-walking plans, and my back was talking to me about it. "Let's go look at the flowers." Taking a breather and then examining the facts with a fresh perspective often did the trick when I'd backed myself into a plot corner with my mystery novels, so why not now? One puzzle was much the same as any other.

We wandered toward the park's flower gardens, brimming with purple salvias, pinks asters, and yellow penstemons, all still blooming as if it was midsummer. Even the bees were laboring, collecting nectar as they would on a warm July day.

"I planted hollyhocks on the south side of my house two years ago," Julia said absentmindedly. "I didn't realize they only lasted two years. It seems such a waste now."

"Plant a perennial like these penstemons," I said, brushing my hand across the tops of the taller blooms. Like Julia, I thought there was little point in tending to a plant that died in two years. Some perennials lasted a decade. Or a lifetime. Time. Julia had waited seven years to be legally rid of the trouble George Foster had caused in her life. "I've read that seven years is the usual amount of time it takes to declare a missing person dead."

"Unless there's a good reason to do it sooner," Julia answered. "But because George stole hundreds of thousands of dollars, a lot of people assumed he was still alive and in hiding." A frown creased her face. "And so he was. I had to wait the full seven years."

"George would know that."

"And Aiden would have found out, as obsessed as he was."

"Is there an online version of the paper?"

"There's a website that reprints stories from smaller northern Colorado papers, but only the top stories of the week."

"Which is exactly what this was," I said. "Above the fold." I set out for the library again, double-timing it with Julia in tow.

"What are we doing now?" she said breathlessly.

"I need to find articles in the Fort Collins paper about Chief Gilroy."

"Slow down." Julia tugged on my arm, bringing me to a stop. "I just remembered. Thirty days before the hearing I had to run a notice in the *Post* saying I was declaring George dead. Thirty days, Rachel."

"Of course. It's the law, isn't it? Notice has to be given."

"And the notice ran in every issue of the Juniper Grove and Fort Collins papers for the whole thirty days."

"That's plenty of time to find out about the hearing, no matter where he was."

"Now," said Julia, her eyes narrowing, "tell me why you need articles about the chief from Fort Collins." There was mild reproof in her voice. Her need to defend Gilroy against all enemies, foreign and domestic, was in full flare.

Knowing I was risking her disapproval, I replied, "Because once and for all, I need to know if I can trust him."

CHAPTER 16

On Gilroy's exit from the Fort Collins police force, articles in that city's paper told a different story than did the *Post*. As a detective, Gilroy had a sterling record. Not a blemish on it. But when he arrested the then-mayor's wife for drunk driving, he hit Fort Collins's political machine like a rubber ball hits a brick wall. Reading the articles, I got the impression Gilroy could have fought and won. Equally, I got the impression that he didn't care to fight. Maybe, like me, he was a refugee from all the friction and agitation of life in a bigger city.

But two months into his new job as Juniper Grove chief, Foster and Dillard stole $300,000. Foster's body was never found, and rumors swirled. Or rather, rumors were manufactured by Jillian Newsome and her paper. And just like that, Gilroy was back in the thick of politics.

Though the political claws were out for Gilroy even before he was hired by the Board of Trustees. Digging up more microfiche copies of the *Juniper Grove Post*, I discovered that the board had hired Officer Chase Hammond one week before Gilroy, and even though Gilroy was Hammond's senior in both rank and age, some on the board thought Hammond would make a fine chief. In the end, the vote for Gilroy was unanimous, but Hammond still had his supporters.

I slowed the Forester, pulled to the curb, and cut my headlights. Jillian Newsome's house was across the road and two houses up—a safe distance, I reasoned, and I had my binoculars with me just in case. Her house was alive with lights, shining through her drapeless windows and glowing with warmth in the dark street. Twice in several minutes I watched her peer out one of the windows, close to the glass, lingering there. Waiting.

For who, I had no idea. But Newsome, ambitious as she was, was always in motion, always plotting, talking, meeting. With everything that had happened over the past few days, she wasn't planning a quiet evening at home. She had machinations to devise, and I was going to uncover them. By spying on her. It was a tactic Newsome herself would approve of—when directed at others, of course.

Julia had believed Gilroy when he told her Tom Ventura had no basis for requesting her arrest, but she knew Ventura to be a sly and conniving man and still feared what he might do to her. Frankly, so did I. Gilroy was losing power in Juniper Grove, and Ventura seemed to be on the rise. Worse, the arrest of Ventura's grandson had only fueled his vindictive nature. To protect Julia, I had to document the Newsome-Ventura-Hammond cabal. If Ventura made another move on Julia, I'd expose them all. At board meetings, in the Fort Collins paper, on the sidewalk outside Town Hall if I had to.

When a car approached from the opposite side of the road, I slid down in my seat. I heard the car's engine shut off, the door slam, and thin footsteps fall. I felt for my camera on the passenger seat and rose slowly until I could see clearly over the dashboard.

A shortish woman with dark bobbed hair approached

the door just as Newsome opened it. Before going inside, the woman turned and looked furtively over her shoulder. Belinda Almond.

"This has got to be a joke," I said aloud. I started the car, and with my lights off, I crept ahead along the curb until I could get a good look through Newsome's windows. Had I been so terribly wrong in my judgment of Belinda? Not only about her affair, but about her relationship with Newsome? I watched as she shed her jacket, slung it over the back of the couch, and then turned on Newsome, shaking a finger at her. She advanced, obviously raising her voice, and to my surprise, Newsome held up her hands.

In a moment, the confrontation was over. Belinda grabbed her jacket and strode for the door. Figuring I could sit in the car and forever wonder what had gone on between the two women or get out, and by doing so make it plain that I was sticking my nose very close to their business, I chose the latter.

Belinda roared out of the house, head down like a charging bull, and almost ran into me on the sidewalk.

"Belinda!" I said, marshaling all the false surprise I could. "What are you doing here?"

Her head jerked. "What does that mean?"

"I didn't expect to see you, that's all."

"I can't talk to people?"

"But this is Jillian Newsome's house."

Glaring at me as though I were suffering from a touch of senility, she said, "I realize where I am, Rachel. Do you?"

Every shred of gentleness in her had disappeared, leaving a coarse and hard Belinda behind. In that moment she reminded me of my old boss in Boston. Hard-nosed and capable of getting everything she wanted. "I was sitting at home, wondering about things, and I wanted to talk to Jillian."

Belinda's hands went to her hips. "About what?"

I considered circling around her, but in her preposterous stance—like a schoolmarm ready to strike—I was sure she'd try to stop me. "What's happened to you, Belinda? I don't understand."

"There's nothing for you to understand. It's none of your business."

I shook my head. "This is very much my business. My friends have had their lives upended. I found a body in my backyard and was treated as a suspect by the woman you were just talking to." I leaned in. "And I've had people I believed lie to me." She knew I meant her. I waited, expecting her to answer my charge, but she simply stared at me, incredulous. "I took a close look at the photograph taken at that benefit party," I added.

Still she said nothing, but I began to see small cracks in her tough facade.

"You make one foolish mistake more than seven years ago and it haunts you for life," she said at last.

"You lied to Julia only this morning."

"No, I very carefully didn't say anything about me and George."

"Which was a lie." I heard Newsome's front door slam and with a sideways glance saw her race toward me, her long brown hair flapping behind her head like a tiny cape.

"You don't understand, Rachel. Please don't follow me again."

Belinda spun on her heels and sprinted for her car, but

I stood my ground. I had wanted to talk to Newsome, and here was my chance.

"You're on my property," she screeched.

Not an auspicious beginning.

"I'm on a public sidewalk, and at least I didn't knock on your door and pop a flash in your face."

"What do you want?"

"I wanted to ask you a few questions."

"Go for it."

Her voice was charged with hostility, but I accepted the challenge. "Did you contact Aiden Dillard or was it the other way around?"

Newsome impatiently tapped a foot.

"I don't suppose it matters," I continued. "Aiden returned to Juniper Grove and you two were in contact. I'm guessing he told you about the notes he wrote. It would explain why your article was so thorough, even though it came out just one day after Aiden taped them to people's doors. How did you know Julia got the same note as the others? She didn't talk to you, and neither did anyone who saw her note."

Newsome sniffed and for a fraction of a second looked away. Realizing she'd just told me my guess was correct, her expression hardened. "You can leave now."

"My pleasure."

She's not half as scary as she likes people to believe, I thought, walking back to my car. She had almost seemed . . . frightened. Frightened and alone. Did she have any friends, or was everyone she knew either a news source or an adversary? Probably the latter. I felt a twinge of pity for her.

On my way home, I drove down Main Street and

decided to stop at Grove Coffee to pick up one of their jelly donuts for breakfast. Their pastries weren't up to Holly's standards, but my sweet tooth was calling me, and I knew from experience it would call me even louder tomorrow morning.

By some miracle—considering I'd skipped dinner—I kept to my plan to buy a single donut, but I only made it as far the sidewalk outside Grove Coffee before I caved and reached into the bag. *Just one bite and I'll save the rest.* I bit with gusto, and the donut's blueberry filling oozed and dropped in a glob onto my jacket. My pale teal jacket.

"Rachel?"

My shoulders rose of their own accord and hunched around my neck. I knew that voice.

"Are you all right?"

I dropped the donut into the bag, planted what was almost certainly a demented grin on my face, and swung back. "Chief Gilroy."

"You said I should call you Rachel, didn't you?" Gilroy's eyes dropped to the glob.

"Jelly," I said.

"I see."

I swiped at the glob with my fingers.

"Hang on." He retrieved a handkerchief from his suit jacket.

"Thank you," I said, brushing hair from my face.

He bit back a grin.

"I just smeared blueberry in my hair, didn't I?" I said, taking his handkerchief.

"Yeah, I'm afraid so. A little on your face too."

"Well, at least I'm not walking around with toilet paper stuck to my shoe."

"Do you normally?"

Lord, he thinks I'm an idiot. An idiot and a slob. "It was a joke."

"Yes, I know."

Gilroy was smiling broadly now, but in a good-natured way, without a hint of ridicule. I was standing there with blueberry filling all over me, and somehow this man made we want to laugh at myself. I wiped my face, cleaned the blueberry from my hair as best I could, and pocketed his handkerchief. "I'll get this back to you tomorrow."

"No rush."

"Thanks again."

"Glad to be of help."

Gilroy gave me a tip of his head and continued on his way. I lingered briefly on the sidewalk, watching him as he walked off. So the stone-faced chief could smile after all. An unpretentious, welcoming smile—my favorite kind. And he looked good in jeans. That was undeniable.

I turned away and fished my car keys from my jacket pocket. *Get a grip on yourself. He isn't your type, and you sure aren't his.*

CHAPTER 17

"Peter gave me the day off, and he and I are eating at La Petite Rose on Sunday," Holly said, wiggling in her chair like an excited puppy dog. "My birthday restaurant. Do you know how long it's been?"

"Exactly one year?" I suggested.

"Funny," Holly said.

"All those eighty-hour weeks running the bakery," I said. "Birthday or not, you deserve a treat." I raised my glass and Julia followed suit. "Happy birthday to Holly."

"A very happy birthday," Julia said. "Now where's our waiter? I want poached eggs, sausages, and pancakes."

"I thought this was *my* celebration breakfast," Holly said.

"It's also a celebration of me not having to fix my own," Julia said, glancing about Wyatt's Bistro. "It's hard work making your own pancakes."

"Which reminds me," Holly said. "Jacob Ventura, the little beast, agreed to work for me on weekends for three months without pay to avoid a serious charge on his record. Boy, am I going to work him."

"When did this happen?" Julia asked.

"Yesterday. Just like that." Holly snapped her fingers. "Chief Gilroy asked me what I thought, I said yes, and he arranged it." She blew over the surface of her coffee and gingerly took a sip. "I was relieved, and so was Peter. There's no court case, we get free help for three months, and Jacob gets to think twice about behaving like a delinquent before he destroys his life."

"Maybe he'll decide he wants to get into the bakery business," I said.

"Not at Holly's Sweets, he won't."

After the waitress took our order, I caught Holly up on my theory that George had returned to Juniper Grove to find out what happened to his money. She sat quietly as she listened, and when I finished, she nodded her agreement. "Money is the only reason that makes sense. Why else would he come back and risk going to prison? George was always more serious about money than anything else, wasn't he, Julia?"

"More serious than he was about me," Julia answered. "I was up until midnight thinking about it. Rachel is right. It's why he came back."

"In his own way, he was still looking out for you," I said.

Staring down at her lap, Julia unfolded and folded her napkin. "He had revenge in mind. Someone cheated him, and that was what he cared about. If he cared about what happened to me, he wouldn't have left in the first place."

For a moment, no one spoke. Then Holly cleared her throat and gently rapped her empty coffee cup on the table. "I call this breakfast meeting of the Juniper Grove Mystery Gang to order."

I laughed.

"Is that what we are now?" Julia said. "A gang?"

"Sounds good, doesn't it?" Holly said. "It came to me first thing this morning."

Julia replied with a slight roll of her eyes.

"So Rachel, do we have one or two murderers in Juniper Grove?" Holly asked, much to the horror of a couple at the next table.

Julia cringed. "Quietly. Everyone's on edge as it is."

I surveyed the other tables in the restaurant. I'd half hoped to see one of my suspects there, but I didn't recognize anyone. "Your pancakes, Julia," I said as our waitress approached balancing an enormous tray on her shoulder.

Orange juice, French toast with strawberries, bacon and eggs, croissants, steaming cups of coffee. It was a feast, and I vowed to invite Julia and Holly here again when my birthday came around. It beat a blueberry donut—which I'd shampooed from my hair last night.

"Let's get down to business," Julia said, talking around a mouthful of syrup-drenched pancake. "When George died, I suspected Aiden, but that doesn't seem right now."

"I'll bet the person who killed George was the person he entrusted with the money," I said. "And Holly, I think we have one murderer, not two."

"Agreed," Holly said.

I sipped my coffee, added a touch more cream, drank again, and then leaned back in my chair. "Here's the problem with that. Who had a motive for killing both men?"

Julia didn't hesitate. "Jillian Newsome is at the top of my list. Tom Ventura is number two. Such a bitter man."

"Officer Hammond," Holly said, glancing around the table. "He wants Chief Gilroy's job, and who knows how far he'd go to get it?"

"Mayor McDermott?" Julia asked.

And Belinda Almond, I added silently.

"What do you think, Rachel?" Holly asked.

"I need a pen and paper," I said.

Holly poked inside her purse and produced a pen and scrap of paper from a small notebook.

I started writing, brainstorming as the ink flowed. "I think this is the sequence of events. It's not exact, but it's close enough." I quickly made my list and then laid the pen on the table. "First, there was the court declaration that George Foster is dead. George and Aiden Dillard found out about that and came back to Juniper Grove, George to find out what happened to his money, and Aiden for revenge. Second, Aiden and Newsome joined forces, each for their own purposes."

Julia raised her hand. "What was Aiden's purpose?"

"To cause as much trouble as he could," I said. "To get as many people as possible at one another's throats. Which is why he showed up at the Farmers' Market Festival. He wasn't supposed to be there, I'm sure of it. He was supposed to keep out of sight at the Lilac Lane, except at night. Aiden's revenge also gave Newsome the headlines she wanted."

"Third?" Holly said, dabbing at the corners of her mouth with a napkin.

"Third, Aiden and Tom Ventura joined forces. Ventura used Aiden for his own purposes, too. Whether he met Aiden before Newsome did or after, I don't know, and I don't think it matters. Aiden's appearance in Juniper Grove presented him and Officer Hammond with an opportunity they couldn't resist."

"Fourth, Aiden and Hammond joined forces," Holly

said.

I reminded Holly that we had never seen Aiden and Hammond together. "But I'm positive Ventura, Hammond, and Newsome are working together."

"To make Chief Gilroy look bad," Julia said.

I sipped at my coffee, trying to recall the conversations I'd heard, the snippets of information in the newspaper, the players in motion on the festival field. Thankfully, the couple at the next table chose that moment to pay their bill and leave, allowing me to raise my voice above a whisper.

"When the court hearing came up," I said, "they knew they could take a case from seven years ago and use it to ruin Gilroy, or at the very least throw doubt on his abilities as a police chief. Ventura, Newsome, and Hammond ended up working together, in their own way, though Ventura thought Newsome was overstepping her bounds. She was supposed to publish articles on Gilroy, that's it. Instead, she got involved with Aiden too, and Ventura knew that could get messy."

"But which one of them killed Aiden and Julia's husband?" Holly asked.

"And who's going to protect Chief Gilroy from those monsters?" Julia said.

"I think he knows who's out to get him," I said. "Not every detail of what they're doing, but he knows."

"Good," Julia declared, rapping the table with her knuckles. "He's worth more than the three of them put together."

"We need more coffee," Holly said, searching for the coffee waiter while shooting me a Julia-is-at-it-again look.

Holly had no idea I was beginning to feel the same as

Julia, and not just because Gilroy looked good in jeans. Not even because he didn't mock me during the Blueberry Donut Incident, though his kind reaction told me much about the man. No, like Julia, I was beginning to think that Gilroy was good for Juniper Grove, maybe even irreplaceable. I wanted him around, like I wanted my friends and my rose bushes around.

"All these people were here during the bank theft," Holly said, waving a hand at a coffee-bearing waiter. "I know I'm stating the obvious, but if they're killers, why didn't they kill before?"

"There was no reason to until George and Aiden came back," I said. "George might have given up the name of the third person, the one who was supposed to give money to Julia."

"Or hurt them, if he thought someone took what was his," Julia said.

I waited for the waitress to refill our coffees before going on. "Aiden was talking to both Newsome and Ventura. Hammond too, I'll bet. It's possible he heard something he wasn't supposed to and one of them discovered that."

"He could have been blackmailing one of them," Julia said. "Poor Aiden."

It seemed to me that Julia could only remember Aiden as the teenager who had been hurt deeply by his father's criminal activity and death. She didn't want to face the fact that he had grown into a man who made his own poor decisions.

"It's a wonder they all haven't been blackmailing each other for years," Holly said. She laughed at the idea. "Maybe they are."

I thought back to the day of the Farmers' Market Festival and the feeling I'd had that the answer to George Foster's murder was in front of me, in the constant movement of suspects—and of victim, as it turned out. "Aiden's appearance at the festival was meant to be a threat to the others. I remember him wandering around the grounds—not like he was looking for something or someone, but like he wanted to be seen. He ran off when he saw me watching, but he wanted Ventura, Newsome, and Hammond to see him. In some strange way, he blames them for his father's death too."

"Well, one of them took him up on his threat." Holly took a last bite of her French toast and washed it down with coffee.

Waiters scrambled to find empty tables as more than a dozen people entered Wyatt's Bistro in the space of two minutes. I watched as an especially boisterous group of four women came in the door, and behind them—my jaw dropped—a reserved-looking Tom Ventura and Officer Hammond. I couldn't believe my luck.

"Don't turn around, you two, but suspects at one o'clock." I told Julia and Holly who it was, describing their somber faces. Ventura and Hammond were going to talk business. Unpleasant business.

"I'm going to hover," I said, balling my napkin and tossing it to my plate.

"Stay right where you are," Julia said.

"They're on the other side of that little art section we saw once—the wall where they display local artists' watercolors. They won't see me."

My eyes on Hammond and Ventura, I edged my way to the watercolors. Engrossed in their menus, they didn't see me, or much of anything else, for that matter. The menu wasn't that riveting, but they were like kids with their earbuds, only not enjoying the music so much as enjoying the distraction that kept them from having to face other people.

I swung wide around their table, inched my way to the wall directly behind them, and pretended interest in a watercolor of the Maroon Bells, two beautiful Colorado peaks.

Nothing. Neither of them said a word. I sidestepped to another watercolor. Ventura grunted.

"What?" Hammond said.

"We never should have told her."

I sidestepped back to the Maroon Bells.

"We didn't tell her," Hammond said. "Aiden Dillard did."

"I still can't believe the little snot put one of his notes on *my* door."

Hammond chuckled. "Better that than you're left out. How would that have looked? Anyhow, Newsome was happy to help."

"She's not a help, Hammond. She's going to ruin everything."

"You should talk. Your going freelance will land us both somewhere we don't want to be."

"I'm trying to move things along."

"By stealing from me?" Hammond hissed. "I invite you over and you steal."

"And what about you?" Ventura's voice faded to a loud whisper. "Why do you think I picked a public place to meet?"

"Are you serious?" Hammond said. "I'm not the one

you have to worry about. Listen to me, we can control Newsome."

"She and her paper run this town."

"That's going to change very soon."

Ventura snorted. "If we get that far. I think Gilroy knows something."

"He won't last long. Newsome will see to that. I'm more worried about that nosy writer, Rachel Stowe. What a pain in the neck she is."

My mouth dropped open. *And I thought you had a friendly smile.*

"She's no threat," Ventura said. "She doesn't have two brain cells to rub together."

My jaw dropped another inch.

"It's beautiful, isn't it?"

I jerked to attention.

"This artist captures the Maroon Bells like no one else." A young woman in dreadlocks came up beside me, admiring the watercolor on the wall.

I closed my mouth and nodded.

"Are you thinking of buying it?"

I shrugged.

"The same artist has an oil color of the Maroons in another part of the restaurant. Would you like me to show you?"

Making an apologetic face, I shook my head.

"He's my friend, so . . . Do you want his card?"

Again I shook my head.

By now she was getting the point. I was a lunatic.

"All right, whatever."

The woman crept off and I strained to hear Ventura and Hammond's voices again. In a few seconds, I was rewarded.

"Have you considered that Newsome is dangerous?" Ventura asked.

"No," Hammond said with confidence. And then, more tentatively, "You think?"

"She's ambitious."

Hammond chuckled. "We're all ambitious."

"I saw her talking to Aiden at the festival, minutes before he died."

"She promised to stay away from him."

"She lied, Hammond. She followed him. And then I followed her—all the way to the knitting tent."

There was a long pause in which neither Hammond nor Ventura said a word. I longed to peer around the wall, to judge the expressions on their faces, but I didn't dare.

"She was talking to McDermott," Ventura finally said. "After a minute, McDermott left and so did I. Newsome stayed behind in the tent."

"Do you think . . . ?" Hammond said.

"That she could drive a knitting needle through a man's neck? Yes, I do."

CHAPTER 18

After I'd summarized Ventura and Hammond's conversation for Julia and Holly, leaving out their pointed criticism of me, I hightailed it out of Wyatt's and drove to the police station, hoping to catch Chief Gilroy before Officer Hammond made it back there. He knew something was going on that wasn't good for his career, but did he know his second-in-command and the town's attorney were in direct contact and working for his ouster?

I found Gilroy at the station's front desk, his nose in some paperwork. Underhill, who was on a computer, looked up when I walked in, announced my name, and went back to his monitor.

"Can I talk to you for a minute?" I asked Gilroy, pointing at an open office door.

"Sure. Underhill, get me that list, and then check with the ME's office for the autopsy on Dillard."

"Where's Hammond?" Underhill said, a hint of complaint in his voice.

"When he gets here, tell him I need to see him."

Gilroy moved for the open door, and when he reached it, he stood aside, letting me enter first. "Have a seat. What can I help you with?"

I couldn't sit. In my compulsion to protect Gilroy, I'd dashed to his office without the faintest idea how to broach the delicate subject of him being the target of at least two town officials. Where to begin?

"Is there something wrong?"

Delicacy aside, he had to know. "I overheard something a little while ago, and I think you should know about it."

"Take a seat, Rachel."

"No, thanks. Maybe you already know this," I said, shoving my hands in my jeans pockets to keep them still, "and I know I mentioned some of it before, but what I heard this morning is absolute confirmation." I paused to gauge his reaction, and in that moment I saw a photo on the wall directly behind his desk. The same photo I'd seen earlier in Tom Ventura's office, of him and Ventura fishing. Enjoying each other's company. I hated to do this. "When was that taken?" I asked, gesturing with my head.

Gilroy glanced over his shoulder. "A few months ago on the Blue River. Why?"

Smiling just a few months ago. So they were still friends. I took a deep breath. "I overheard Tom Ventura and Officer Hammond talking about you."

Gilroy eyed me suspiciously.

"It's clear they and Newsome are plotting to remove you from office, and Hammond wants to take your place as chief of police."

"I asked you not to investigate."

"I overheard them at a restaurant. That's not investigating."

"You just happened to overhear them?"

"Sort of."

"You didn't make an effort of any kind?"

"I was with my friends for Holly Kavanagh's

birthday. We didn't know Hammond and Ventura were going to be there. As it turns out, I was pretty lucky to—"

"Rachel." Gilroy was shaking his head. Hard. He stood, and I knew our conversation was coming to a swift end.

"You know all of this, don't you?" I said. "Why don't you do something?"

"You can't arrest people for wanting your job."

But it was more than three people wanting to dethrone the chief and make Juniper Grove their little kingdom. Two people dead, the vandalism of my friend's bakery, a newspaper editor who used the power of the press to intimidate. In my mind I saw Belinda Almond again, filled with rage and storming from Newsome's house. "Everyone says they dislike Newsome, but they all talk with her. Why is that?"

"Not talking to her doesn't work, as you know. Are we finished here? Because I have two murders on my hands."

"How would you react if you were being blackmailed?"

He moved around his desk. "I'd be angry."

"Would you confront your blackmailer?"

"Probably. Are you being blackmailed?"

"Not me. What if . . . ?" I clamped my mouth shut. I had no proof of what I was thinking, and the last thing I needed was more of Gilroy's disapproval.

"Stop investigating, Rachel. That's my job."

"You're welcome," I said.

He spread his hands in confusion. "What am I supposed to thank you for?"

I left his office without another word and marched off

to my car. *What an infuriating man!* One minute he was kind, the next minute he was making me feel like an intruder. "Not a single thank-you," I mumbled as I started my car. Granted, I was on his turf, but I was genuinely trying to help. He'd never even asked me what Hammond and Ventura had said.

Minutes later I was on Glen Haven Road, looking for a house with a blue minivan in the driveway. I was sticking my nose in things again, but for some reason my conscience was prodding me to help Belinda. There was no excuse for her probably brief affair with George Foster, but despite her lies, she seemed deeply sorry for what she'd done to Julia. And now she was in Newsome's clawlike hands.

My guess was Newsome had incriminating evidence against Belinda, possibly in the form of more photos from the benefit party. Question was, what was Newsome getting from Belinda in return for not publishing them? Newsome didn't need money—I'd seen her house and car—but she craved information and the power over people's lives that it gave her.

As I made my way up the paving-stone walk to Belinda's mock Tudor house, I silently practiced my greeting, hoping that she didn't think my arrival was outrageously intrusive. I rapped on the door and waited.

A shadow passed over the peephole, and a second later Belinda flung open the door. "Rachel. You found me."

"I need to talk to you, Belinda."

She waved me in, shut the door behind me, then pivoted back. "I didn't think I'd see you again."

"I'm sorry to bother you."

"What I mean is, I didn't think I'd see you after I was

so nasty. Come on back."

I followed Belinda from her foyer to her kitchen. Counting the small dining area at one end, the kitchen was as large as the first floor of my house, and it was startlingly white: white walls, white pendant lights, and white marble on every counter, including the enormous center island. Maybe I was wrong about Newsome not taking Belinda's money. She seemed to have plenty of it.

While the rest of the kitchen was pristine, the round table in the dining area was in use, covered with issues of the *Juniper Grove Post*, dirty plates, and used teacups. Belinda cleared the newspapers and motioned for me to sit. "Can I get you a cup of tea?" she asked, making her way to the sink.

"Sure, thanks."

Belinda shot me a tight-lipped smile over her shoulder. "I take it you have something you want to say and I'm not going to want to hear it." She plugged in an electric kettle and leaned back against the counter.

"There's no sense beating around the bush," I said. "I know Jillian Newsome is blackmailing you." It was a stab in the dark, without any proof, but I felt things were about to come to a bad ending and I didn't have time to fool around.

"What?" she cried, waving her small hands in front of her. "How? How did you know? Did she tell you?" She abandoned the kettle and joined me at the table.

"I didn't talk to her, I promise."

"How did you know?"

"Why else would you be meeting with her? You can't stand her."

Belinda propped her elbows on the table and

massaged her temples with her hands. "I don't know what to do."

"Has she been blackmailing you for seven years?"

"Only five days."

It was my turn to be shocked. "Over George Foster?"

She laughed ruefully. "Didn't I say one mistake can haunt you for years?"

Hearing the electric kettle on the boil, Belinda headed for the counter and drew a box of teabags from the cabinet. She brought two cups to the table, carefully setting mine in front of me before again taking her seat.

"Why would Newsome blackmail you after all these years?" I asked.

"She came to my house the morning after I got one of those anonymous notes and said that George being declared dead changed everything. She needed a heftier newspaper—that's what she called it—and with the court hearing on George and my help, she was going to get it."

"She didn't ask you for money."

"Not money, no." Her eyes began to glisten with tears. "She wanted information on what people were saying about George Foster."

"What people?"

"Mostly Chief Gilroy and Julia Foster." She hastily brushed away tears before they fell.

I couldn't believe my ears. I stared at Belinda, waiting for her to say something else, something in her own defense besides "I was being blackmailed." Gilroy, I understood, a little, but Julia?

"You think I'm horrible."

"Julia gave you a hand in friendship, even though—"

"I know, I know, but I didn't tell Newsome anything,

I swear. She asked me if Julia ever hinted that George left her money, and I said no, the opposite, and I told her that I knew Julia didn't want anything to do with George or his memory. When she pressed me for more, I made up things, like Julia always liked Aiden and didn't care that George was dead. Newsome got mad at me because I didn't give her anything negative about Julia that she could print."

"What did you say about Gilroy?"

"I made things up about him too."

"Like?"

"Like he and his two officers fought all the time. She was pleased with that, so I gave her more. I said I knew a cop in Fort Collins who said Gilroy was a corrupt detective and set people up for DUIs."

"Oh, Belinda . . ." Sick at heart, I got up from the table.

"I don't know what to do," I heard her say again.

I wheeled back on her. "You've hurt innocent people. You make it right."

"It's too late."

"Did Newsome ask you who this Fort Collins cop was?"

"I told her I couldn't say."

"She took your word for it?"

"You've seen the *Juniper Grove Post*. All she needs to write is 'Our sources say' or 'Sources tell us' and she protects herself from libel." She stood and began to nervously clear the table.

"But it *is* libel—or slander," I said, refusing to back off. "You're not legally in the clear, Belinda. You have to make it right. What you said about Julia is bad enough, but Chief Gilroy could lose his reputation and even his job."

Dropping our teacups in the sink, Belinda heaved a sigh and turned back to me. “Fixing it is easier said than done.”

“Do you have proof she’s blackmailing you?”

“She was stupid enough to email me. She’s so sure of herself.”

“Then you can stop her. It won’t be easy, but if you tell the truth, you’ll be free of Jillian Newsome.”

“I’ll lose my house!” Belinda cried. “My husband cheated on me five years ago. We divorced, and I ended up with this house. If he finds out I cheated on him first, I’ll lose everything.”

“He didn’t believe the rumors about you and George?”

“Never.”

“Then he won’t believe them now, when Newsome produces whatever she has on you.”

“She has more photos from the benefit party.”

“The one in the paper wasn’t bad.”

“That was the least compromising one. The photographer snapped it when George was being a drunken jerk. Trust me, Rachel, if my husband sees the other photos—and Newsome will publish them or mail them to him—he’ll believe the rumors.”

“That party was more than seven years ago. Why would your husband do—”

“He resents giving up the house. End of story.”

I made my way to the front door, wondering how Jillian Newsome, that menace of a woman, could live in my beautiful little town for all these years and yet still want to bully its residents. Or worse than bully. Anyone who would keep photographs for seven years on the off chance she could blackmail someone with them was not a well woman. But was she capable of murder?

Belinda followed, and we stood together in the foyer as I searched for a way to make a graceful exit. She looked so miserable at that moment that I wished I had something encouraging to say to her, even knowing what she'd done to Julia and Gilroy.

I paused, my hand on the door knob. "Is there anything else you can tell me that might help?"

Belinda shrugged. "I told Newsome I heard Officer Hammond and Tom Ventura arguing at the festival."

"Did you make that up?"

"No, it's the truth. I also told her I saw Mayor McDermott and Ventura arguing—and that's the truth."

"You say you *heard* Hammond and Ventura arguing. Did you catch what they were they saying?"

"Some of it. Hammond told Ventura he was an idiot and he was going to end up ruining everything by going freelance."

"Freelance?" That word again. What did Hammond mean?

"That's what he said. Then Ventura said something like, 'How was I supposed to know? You're the cop.' Then he said Gilroy was too stupid to notice anyway. That's about it."

"No idea of what they were talking about?"

"No, sorry."

"All right, thank you."

Belinda pushed on the door, preventing me from opening it. "One more thing. I'm afraid I said something about you." She watched me expectantly, judging whether she should go on, I thought, or waiting for me to deliver her from her discomfort by telling her that whatever she'd told Newsome was just peachy. "Newsome said you were looking into George Foster's murder so you could sell more books, and I told her you were on the verge of solving the case."

"Tell me you're joking."

"I'm so, so sorry." Her hands shaking, she reached into her jeans pocket and pulled out a white box with green lettering on the front. "They make it look like a cigarette pack," she said. "Isn't that insane?"

"What is it?"

"Nicotine gum."

"You smoke?"

"I used to. Now I'm hooked on the gum." She popped the square in her mouth.

"I've seen that pack before." I took it from her hands and covered the lower portion of it with my palm so that only half the lettering showed. "Only I thought it was an embroidered handkerchief."

CHAPTER 19

For the first time in days, I felt a real sense of fear. For a minute, sitting in my car outside Belinda's house, I was almost paralyzed with it. I was knee-deep in trouble now. It was bad enough that George Foster had been killed in my backyard, but now the killer thought I was on to him. Or her.

I was now sure Tom Ventura had dropped a cigarette in my yard to make Gilroy look incompetent, but had he murdered Foster and Aiden Dillard? Something told me he wasn't capable. Ventura was on the periphery, trying to hurry the process of getting rid of Gilroy so he could be mayor, but talking with Hammond at Wyatt's Bistro, he sounded like a man who feared things were spiraling out of control.

As soon as I got home, I checked the outdoor lights at the front and back of my house and made sure the deadbolts and chain locks were serviceable. Living in Juniper Grove, I'd become sloppy with my security, hardly using the deadbolts and leaving the chains dangling all the time. Not that a cheap chain would stop a killer.

If Newsome had killed Foster or Aiden, she'd try to silence me. If she hadn't killed them, she'd spread word to Hammond, Ventura, and the whole rotten crew that I was about to name the killer, and one of them would come after me. No way was I going to call Gilroy to let him know I was a target. He'd tell me it was my own fault.

"Time to get deadly serious," I said out loud as I riffled through the refrigerator for something to eat. "Treat this like the plot of a mystery novel." Ignoring part of a leftover cream puff in one of Holly's pink boxes, I grabbed a hunk of cheese, sandwich bread, and cold cuts and dropped them onto a large plate. Feeling virtuous, I jogged up the stairs to my writing room.

My computer desk faced a giant corkboard I used to plot my mysteries—a place to jot down ideas, display drawings and photos of my imagined characters and locations, come up with connections between events to flesh out my plots. I hated pulling down all my work, but I set to it, leaving nothing behind but a few dozen thumbtacks. Then I began to rebuild the corkboard with an altogether different mystery in mind.

Twenty minutes later I had the basics before me. The victims, the suspects, the motives, the opportunities. And the blackmail. I stuck Gilroy's name up there for good measure. He was connected to all the suspects in some way, except maybe Belinda, and he was the reason Hammond, Ventura, and Newsome were cooperating with one another.

I threw together a sandwich, sat at my desk, and stared at the corkboard. The clues to George Foster's death lay in the past, in the events surrounding his and Mitch Dillard's bank theft. Dillard had died within hours of the theft on the rapids of the Blue River, but Foster may as well have died the same day. It was only a matter of time before fate and his killer caught up with him.

It still puzzled me that George had dug a hole in my backyard the night he was killed. Surely it wasn't to retrieve an old piece of paper that read, "Chief Gilroy is a liar." A liar about what? I tried to imagine the sequence of events: George crept into my yard, the killer was waiting for him, and . . . No, it couldn't have happened that way. George and his killer arrived together—it had to be—and one or both of them dug that hole.

Evening was still a few hours away, so I called Julia over with the promise of homemade pancakes after church next Sunday. My thoughts were going in aimless circles and I needed her sensible and fresh pair of eyes.

"This is a war room," she said when she saw my corkboard. "In all the months you've lived here, I've never seen where you write." She glanced at what remained of my sandwich, clucking her tongue. "That's a meal?"

"And it was delicious." I took her by the shoulders and positioned her in front of the corkboard. "Tell me what you see."

"A lot of pieces of paper."

"Obviously. What else?"

"Why is Belinda Almond's name up there? Is she a suspect?"

"Everyone's a suspect," I said, sidestepping the real issue.

"Well . . ." Julia tilted her head to the left. Then the right. "All of these people knew George seven years ago."

"And except for Mayor McDermott, they all held the same position back then as they do today. Officer Hammond was Officer Hammond, Chief Gilroy was Chief Gilroy, Tom Ventura was the town attorney, Jillian Newsome was the editor in chief of the *Post*."

Julia searched my eyes. "What was Belinda Almond?"

"Just Belinda. A sad woman."

"Yes?"

"Unlike you, Julia." I shoved my hands in my pockets and stared at the board. "Is it possible that one of these people was supposed to give you some of George's money?"

"Let's see." She pointed at the board. "*Not* Chief Gilroy."

"Of course."

"Why do you dislike him?"

"I don't. Really. Seriously, I don't."

Julia let out a gentle, between-friends laugh. "You *like* him."

"What? Stop it."

"Don't deny it. I'm old enough to know the signs. You can't talk about him without becoming irritated."

"Since when is irritation a sign of affection?"

"Since Adam and Eve."

"Let's get back to this corkboard," I said, trying to pull both our heads out of the clouds. There was no point in thinking about James Gilroy, chief of police. Ice blue eyes, dark hair. I wasn't in his ballpark. "Anyway, I'm sure he has a girlfriend."

"I've seen him with a date."

"See?"

Her hands flew to her hips. "He's not supposed to date?"

Well, I don't date, I wanted to say. Time to shift the subject back to murder. "Think, Julia. Which one of our suspects might George have trusted with some of the stolen money?"

She exhaled loudly and refocused on the corkboard.

"He and Tom Ventura didn't get along." She pointed at Gilroy's and Hammond's names. "And he didn't like the police."

"What about Newsome?"

"Like everyone else in Juniper Grove, he didn't like her or trust her."

"McDermott?"

"He didn't dislike him, but he didn't really know him." She stepped closer to the board. "What about Belinda?" Julia spun around, her hand to her throat. "What if the money wasn't even for me? What if he left it for Belinda?"

"Remember, it was news of the court hearing that brought both George and Aiden back to town, and there was nothing in the hearing about Belinda. She wasn't in court and she wasn't in the papers."

Julia relaxed and dropped her hand. "I had an awful thought that . . ."

"Belinda has plenty of money. She does now and she did then."

"Then who?"

"George must have been friendly with one of these people. Maybe you didn't know how he felt."

"That's more than possible." Julia wandered over to my desk chair and sat. "You were always leaving messes behind you, George."

I planted myself in front of the corkboard and stared at it as though it held the answers, and in a way, it did. The answers were there in front of me, I just couldn't see clearly enough to untangle the clues from the insignificant details. "I forgot the cigarette I found in my backyard," I said, writing "cigarette" on a sticky note and placing it under Ventura's name. "Officer Underhill said the chief was looking at it as if it meant something to him. I think I know why now."

"Nothing ever came of it."

"Gilroy isn't saying anything, but I think Tom Ventura dropped it. Ventura is trying to quit smoking and probably has cigarettes around the house. He left a cigarette at the crime scene to make Gilroy look bad. That's what Hammond meant by 'freelancing.' Ventura wanted to speed things up and broke with the plan."

"He was always a foolish man."

"I hate to say this, but there are two people who could have taken the money, or some of it, from George."

Julia glowered at the corkboard.

"Who could have found George on the day he and Mitch Dillard stole that money and never told a soul?" I asked.

A moment later, Julia realized what I was saying. "Chief Gilroy isn't dirty, Rachel. Hammond, maybe, but not Gilroy."

"Think about it. They found Dillard's body but never found George, alive or dead. George had the money."

Julia was shaking her head. "Hammond, maybe."

"George came back to find out why you never got your part of the money, to stop running and face the music, whatever. They couldn't allow that."

"Hammond couldn't allow that."

Julia was right. The man I knew, however briefly I'd known him, as Chief James Gilroy would never steal hundreds of thousands of dollars and bash a man's head in with a shovel. Or put a knitting needle in his neck. But Officer Chase Hammond was a different man altogether.

"Remember this morning, when I was eavesdropping on Ventura and Hammond? I told you they were arguing, but Ventura said he'd deliberately arranged to meet Hammond in a public place. He was *afraid* of him."

Julia's eyes grew large. "Officer Hammond is the killer."

"We have zero proof." Again I studied the board. "Court hearing," I said, counting off on my fingers, "Aiden's notes, the newspaper articles, hole dug, George killed, buried box found, cigarette found, Aiden killed." I let out a little roar of frustration. "I'm not getting anywhere. I need to clear the cobwebs." I twisted back to Julia. "Want one-quarter of an old cream puff?"

"I wouldn't say no. Even if you did phrase it so I would."

Downstairs in the kitchen, I took the Holly's Sweets box from my fridge and tried to remove the leftover cream puff without damaging it—quite the operation, considering that the cream filling had oozed and glued itself to the box. I ended up using a spatula to free it.

"You weren't joking," Julia said.

"Nothing wrong with it, though. Holly says that if they're refrigerated, they're safe for three days."

"I hope she has a wonderful time tonight. She works too hard."

"It's not work if you love it, and she loves that bakery. It's a shame Jacob Ventura vandalized it, even if she is getting a free employee for the next three months."

"He never said why he broke in." Julia took her plate, examined her damaged slice of cream puff, and decided she would chance taking a bite.

"Tom Ventura doesn't like Holly. He made that very

clear the first day I met him. I think Jacob picked up on that and was trying to please his grandfather."

"Mmm."

"I want another look at the hole in my yard. Coming?"

I strode into the backyard with Julia in tow, half expecting to find another cigarette or some other evidence that my privacy had been invaded again.

"When are you going to fill that in?" Julia asked.

"I'm thinking of planting a tree." I did a half circle around the hole, hoping to catch something I'd missed before.

"Do you think a woman could dig a hole in this hard clay?"

"I've dug back here." I pointed to my left, at a climbing rose rising up latticework along the fence. "I planted that right after I moved in. I added amendments to the soil so the roots could breathe."

Julia's eyes were drawn to the cedar gate on the west side of my yard. "I see a woman's hand waving," she said.

"Hello!" Holly called out.

Cupping my hands around my mouth, I shouted, "Come in!"

"I rang the doorbell, but no one answered," Holly said, shutting the gate. "Then I thought I heard you back here."

"We need another pair of eyes," I said, glad for her company. While I sometimes read too much into things or complicated them, Holly was the opposite, seeing simplicity in apparent chaos.

"What are we looking at?" she asked.

"The hole," I said, pointing.

"Okay."

"We had a leftover cream puff," Julia said as the three of us stared. "Rachel had to pry it from the box."

Goodness knows what my other neighbors would have thought, had they seen us congregating around a hole in the ground. At that moment I was especially grateful for my fence.

"A hole is a hole," Julia said. "The police have never figured out why George would dig it just to stick a box in it."

And then it hit me. "The bakery box, of course!" Why hadn't I seen it before? Standing there, looking at the clay soil, thinking of the rain we'd had and the snow to come, it was embarrassingly obvious. "Gilroy figured it out. So did Hammond, I'm sure, and I'll bet even Officer Underhill had a lightbulb go off eventually."

"About the hole?" Holly asked.

"About the piece of paper and box. Julia, are you positive that was George's handwriting on the paper?"

"One hundred percent."

"The night we found George, you told Hammond he could search your house again, that the police had searched it several times before."

"I was exaggerating. They searched it twice."

"And you said George liked to scribble letters to the editor. By hand?"

"Always. It gave him more satisfaction."

"What if that strip of paper in the box Underhill found was torn from one of George's letters?" I asked.

Julia considered. "It did look like one of his letters. But I can't understand why he'd tear off part of it and bury it back here."

"He didn't."

"I'm sure that was his writing."

"It was his handwriting, but someone found a letter he'd written and tore off the bottom strip, leaving a single incriminating line and George's signature."

"By 'someone' you mean a cop," Holly said. "A cop buried that box in your yard."

"At Wyatt's, Hammond said Ventura had stolen from him. I think Hammond took the letter, thinking he might use it later, and at some point he showed it to Ventura. Then Ventura, trying to hurry Gilroy's ouster, tore the strip from the bottom of the letter and left it in the box."

"They planned this years ago?" Julia said.

"No, days ago." I threw my head back, frustrated by my failure to spot such a glaring clue. "I should have seen it! Even the box from Holly's Sweets started to fall apart when the cream filling touched it. Cardboard doesn't last, and I distinctly remember Underhill saying he found the paper in a cardboard box. After seven years, there would be little left of a cardboard box or the paper in it."

"I see what you mean," Holly said. "Who would be stupid enough to bury cardboard and pretend it lasted seven years in the ground?"

"I can tell you one thing," I replied with certainty. "It wasn't a cop. Any detective or street cop would know better. It was a civilian."

CHAPTER 20

"I need to drive downtown before everything closes for the day," I said, heading into the house for my car keys. "Anyone game?"

"You bet I am," Julia said, coming to a halt at the back door.

I locked the door and turned to Holly. "I know it's your birthday, but—"

"You're onto something," Holly said, grinning wildly, "and you are not leaving me behind."

One minute later we were in my Forester driving down Finch Hill Road for Main Street.

Holly checked her phone for messages, asked if we could stop by the bakery first, and then hit a quick-dial number.

Julia leaned forward in the back seat and said quietly, "Maybe Peter needs her help."

"What?" Holly shouted into her phone. "Where did he do it? At her office? Oh, I'd pay money to see that." She held the phone away from her ear. "It's Peter. He's hearing from customers that Gilroy just arrested Jillian Newsome."

I hit the brake, causing Holly to throw out her free hand and catch herself on the dashboard.

"What's Gilroy up to?" I said. "She's not the killer. It can't be her."

Julia leaned forward again, grabbing on to the back of my seat. "If you had seen her with those knitting needles, you might think differently."

"Could you have it wrong?" Holly said gently, pocketing her phone. "You kinda solved the cardboard box thing—that's pretty good."

"I should have solved that the second I heard about it."

"Chief Gilroy wouldn't arrest someone on a whim," Julia said. "He knows what he's doing."

I rolled my eyes. "I know, he's perfect."

"Not quite, but close," Julia said, smiling smugly.

"Can we still stop at the bakery?" Holly said. "I want to see how Peter's doing."

I pressed down on the accelerator. "And I want to hear what he's heard."

We entered Holly's Sweets during what Peter said was only his second lull of the day. "Has everyone gone crazy for donuts?" he asked of no one in particular as he scrubbed away at a blotch near the register.

"Possibly, honey," Holly said, working her way around the counter. "But for now we need to know exactly what you heard about Newsome's arrest."

"Huh?" Peter let go of his sponge and for the first time seemed to notice there were three of us in the bakery, all eagerly awaiting his report. "Oh, sure. Let's see. It happened an hour ago, at the newspaper office. People saw Gilroy taking her into custody, putting her in his cruiser."

"Was she handcuffed?" Julia asked.

"From what people are saying, yes."

"Wow," Holly exclaimed. "I never thought I'd see the day."

I stepped close to the counter. "Peter, this is very important. What are the charges against Newsome?"

He lifted his shoulders. "Murder, I guess, but no one seems to know for sure."

"I wonder if it will be in the paper tomorrow," Holly said. "Wouldn't that be ironic?"

As much as I disliked Jillian Newsome, I didn't believe she was the killer. She had nothing to gain by murdering Foster and Aiden. On the contrary, they were valuable to her as sources of information and subjects of her news articles. Now that they were both dead, interest in them would soon fade, and her dreams of a heftier paper along with it. "This is wrong," I said.

"You're unhappy that Newsome was arrested?" Julia said, baffled by my remark.

"There are a lot of things you could arrest that woman for, but murder isn't one of them."

"Gilroy should arrest Ventura and Hammond while he's at it," Holly said.

"I wish he could," I said. "Then again . . ." Gilroy had told me he couldn't arrest someone for wanting his job. True enough. But he *could* arrest someone for tampering with a crime scene. Twice. "I'll be back. I need to talk to Gilroy."

"Gilroy?" Holly shouted as I darted out of the bakery.

The pieces were coming together. In a search of Julia's house, Hammond had stolen one of George Foster's letters for later use against Gilroy, and Ventura, impatient to become mayor, took it and clumsily planted part of it as evidence. Later, he dropped a cigarette in my backyard as proof that Gilroy was an amateur. Not being a complete fool, Ventura probably hadn't smoked it, but only let it burn for a while before putting it out and dropping it in my yard.

I slowed my steps as I came to the Juniper Grove Town Hall, cupped my hands around my eyes, and peered through the glass door. It was hard for me to fathom the level of hate that would cause Ventura to chance losing everything—his career and even his freedom—in order to bring down Chief Gilroy. If it wasn't hate, it was ambition on a level I'd never seen.

Ventura had to have known that Officer Hammond was a killer. That Hammond had found George Foster that day on the Blue River and taken some or all of his money, probably with the promise that he'd give some of it to Julia if George left Juniper Grove forever and never returned.

With all my certainty about Ventura and Hammond, something niggled at the edge of my thoughts. I sensed that I was missing the full picture, and I needed to talk to Gilroy. At the very least he was wrong about Newsome.

"Hello, Miss Nosy."

At the sound of Officer Hammond's voice I tried to wheel back, but he pressed in close behind me, pushed opened the glass door, and shoved me inside.

"How dare you!" I screamed.

"We're going to settle your nosiness once and for all."

He grabbed my arm, and as he dragged me toward Tom Ventura's office, I screamed again, hoping to draw attention from any of the offices in the hall, but the only door to open was Ventura's.

"What's going on out there?" he said. "Hammond? What are you doing?"

I broke free of Hammond's grip, but as I spun back,

he grabbed my wrist, dragged me into Ventura's office, and slammed the door shut.

"She's the one who got Newsome arrested," Hammond said, pointing an accusatory finger at me.

"Don't be ridiculous," I protested. As bad as my situation was, I felt relief at being inside Ventura's office. Hammond wasn't crazy enough to murder me in front of the town attorney. *You can talk your way out of this*, I thought.

"Did you know Officer Hammond stole that bank money from George Foster seven years ago?" I said. I was going to throw as much bewildering, and hopefully maddening, information at Ventura as I could. "He found Foster alive by the river, took at least some of his money—maybe all of it—and then let him go. They struck a deal. Foster gets to escape, and Hammond keeps all or most of the money."

Hammond was glaring at me, his jaw halfway to the floor.

"Foster had no choice. It was either agree to the deal or you take him in."

"Is that right, Officer Hammond?" Ventura asked.

"Shut up, Tom," Hammond replied.

"All Foster asked was that Julia get some of the money. Just a little, I think. Right, Officer?" Taking a few small backward steps, I began to put distance between myself and Hammond. "But then there was the court hearing, and George Foster found out Julia had no money. So he came back to Juniper Grove."

Hammond's eyebrows shot up. "What? It's . . . wh—what?" he stammered. "How do you know that?"

"You're right about her being nosy," Ventura said.

"But she's clever too."

I took another backward step, this time toward the office door. "Foster had nothing to lose. He'd been on the run for years, probably had no money left, and his wife had been cheated out of her part of the money. So Hammond killed him."

"What?" Hammond roared with laughter. "You're out of your mind."

Ventura's eyes darkened. "Is she?"

The question brought an abrupt end to Hammond's laughter. He turned on Ventura. "Don't ask me that in front of her. You know I didn't kill anyone."

"Do I?"

"Knock it off."

"I think Rachel is onto something," Ventura said. "You had every reason to kill Foster."

"I took his money, I didn't kill him."

"If you didn't, who did?"

Hammond raked a hand through his hair. "Was it Newsome? Gilroy just arrested her. What about Julia Foster?"

It was Ventura's turn to laugh. "Julia Foster? She hit her husband in the head with a shovel? And I suppose she stuck a knitting needle in Aiden Dillard's neck."

"You thought Newsome did that," Hammond said. "That's what you said. But it was you, wasn't it?"

"Me? So says the dirty cop."

"You ran up to me, told me you saw Newsome talking to Dillard at the festival and he was going to send us all to prison if we didn't stop him. Later you told me you saw *her* with the knitting needles in the tent, but it was you." Hammond was jabbing a finger at Ventura, his anger growing. "You did it."

"I didn't have the time," Ventura said.

"Yes, you did. You practically ran to the tent—I saw you. It took ten seconds. You came back out with a needle, right? What did you do, stick it up your sleeve? Ask Aiden to meet you behind the tent? I'll bet Newsome knew what you were going to do. Did she?"

"Is this all for Rachel's benefit? She knows what you've done, Hammond."

If they started arguing, I thought, I could make my escape. They wouldn't notice I'd reached the office door until it was too late. "You're not blameless in this, Tom," I said. "You planted that cardboard box and the cigarette."

"Oh, man," Ventura said, rubbing his forehead. "You *are* nosy."

"She's got that right too," Hammond said.

"Planting evidence isn't murder or anything close to it," I said. "But if you allow Hammond to continue killing, you'll pay a price."

"I told you I didn't kill anyone!" Hammond shouted.

"You're scaring her, Hammond," Ventura said. "And frankly, you're scaring me."

Hammond had backed himself against a bookcase, and his face and the tops of his ears had gone red. "This is nuts. *You're* nuts, Ventura. You wanted to be mayor that much? It was so important that you had to kill two men?"

"The dirty cop speaks again."

I was getting a bad, bad feeling. Had I misjudged both men?

"You called Foster a loose end," Hammond said. "You said a dead man was going to send me to prison. And if that happened, Gilroy would still be chief, Newsome would be run out of town, and your plan to be mayor of this little burg, with all of us serving you like worker bees, would be ruined. You were trying to get me to kill Foster so you didn't have to."

"You really are scaring me."

"I'll tell you about scary. You were afraid I'd tell Gilroy you knew about Foster's money.

"You're the one who told me, Hammond."

"Prison was in your future, too."

"Tell me how you got old George into Rachel's backyard," Ventura said. "That must have taken some doing. After all, you cheated the man. Why would he follow you?"

I edged closer to the door.

"Did you tell him you'd buried some of *his* money back there and he could have it if he wanted?" Ventura went on. "That it had been there all along?"

"I was on patrol that night."

"That's right, you were on patrol. Which means you could have been anywhere. Did you tell Foster you left Julia's money in Rachel's yard but you needed his help to dig it up because of an old injury?" Ventura grimaced and put a hand to his back, feigning pain.

The hairs on the back of my neck stood straight. I recalled the look I'd seen on Ventura's face at the festival, when he was standing by the flagpole. Shock. Anger. I remembered how quickly he'd disappeared. And I remembered Newsome smiling at Aiden, nodding at him.

"Did you really have to kill them?" Hammond asked. "Just to clean up loose ends?"

Ventura slowly slid open his desk drawer.

"Don't play games," Hammond said.

"It's not a game. I told you, you're scaring me."

Tell her you're afraid of her, Ventura had said to me. *Start setting up your defense*. "It was you," I said, gaping at Ventura. "You killed Foster and Aiden, and you're laying out your defense. You're opening your drawer so Hammond will draw his gun."

Hammond put a hand to his holster but left it there. "Back pain? If there's one thing I know about you, Ventura, it's that you don't have an imagination. You're remembering, not imagining."

I moved closer to the door until I was nearly able to reach the knob.

"I'm only guessing," Ventura said.

"You're telling us what you did—showing off," Hammond said. "You can't resist. Take your hand off the drawer. *Now*. I know you keep your weapon there."

"I'm telling you I'm afraid of you," Ventura said. "You're a murderer and I'm afraid for my life."

Hammond palmed the handle of his pistol and flicked open the safety strap with his thumb. "Don't do it, Ventura. Rachel's a witness."

"Maybe yes, maybe no," Ventura said.

From somewhere in the hall I heard a pounding noise, followed by Chief Gilroy shouting my name. For one brief second, Hammond turned his face to the door and Ventura took his hand off the drawer.

"I'm here!" I grabbed the doorknob and yanked open the door, flinging myself into the hall.

CHAPTER 21

It took twenty minutes and a hot cup of coffee in the Juniper Grove Police Station before I could stop shaking. To his credit, Chief Gilroy never once reminded me that I wasn't a detective and could have gotten myself killed. Better than that, he asked me—only half-jokingly—if I'd ever considered becoming a detective. Then he offered me a ride home, telling me questions about "the incident" could wait until the morning.

"My car's less than two blocks away," I told him. I could have kicked myself. A ride home would have been lovely, but when it came to James Gilroy, my brain seemed constantly on the fritz.

"Your friends are in the lobby," he said.

"Great." It was late, and I was exhausted, eager to sleep without fear of finding an intruder or another body in my backyard. Thankfully, Ventura had rushed to confess to both murders, telling Gilroy that I'd gotten most of it right—about the box and letter and Hammond's theft, if you could call it that, of Foster's stolen money. What I'd missed was that it was Jacob, not he, who dropped Tom's old cigarette in my yard. Willingly. To help his grandfather.

"I can't believe Ventura threw his grandson under the bus," I said. "Implicating him in this conspiracy."

"That's Tom."

"Then you knew what a rat he was?"

Gilroy's shoulders rose in a shrug.

"And you knew that cigarette was Tom's."

"I thought so. I just didn't have enough to go on. I knew he'd been trying to quit, but I also knew he had cigarettes around his office and that was his brand."

I took a long sip of coffee. I felt the night, and my conversation, drawing to a close, but I didn't want either to end. "So you went to the bakery?" I asked. "Is that where you found Holly and Julia?"

"No, they were on the sidewalk outside the bakery. They said you were looking for me and you'd been gone too long. Mrs. Foster said if I didn't do something fast, she'd be forced to change her opinion of me."

I laughed. "That's Julia."

"You have good friends. Worth more than gold." Gilroy stood and stretched his back, signaling it was time for me to go.

I set my Styrofoam coffee cup on his desk and, still somewhat shaky, got to my feet. "Wait a minute. What about Jillian Newsome?"

"What about her?"

"You arrested her, but she didn't murder anyone, even if she did stare at knitting needles at the festival. Newsome stares at everything."

"You thought I arrested her for murder?"

"Yes! I was coming to tell you that you were wrong."

Gilroy let out a boom of a laugh.

"Oh, very funny. What did you arrest her for?"

Suddenly he was his silent self again.

"Come on, everyone will know by tomorrow morning."

Agreeing that I wasn't getting much of an early scoop, he relented. "I arrested her for extortion."

"You're joking."

"That's all I'm going to say."

"Wow. Does this have to do with Belinda Almond?"

Gilroy groaned. "Rachel, what have you gotten into now?"

"Nothing." I waved my hands as if to declare my innocence. "I'm not getting into anything."

"Keep it that way, please," he said, holding open his office door.

I could tell he didn't believe me, but in his expression I saw something more than a gentle warning. It was almost . . . curiosity?

"Mrs. Foster, Mrs. Kavanagh," Gilroy said, tipping his head as we entered the lobby.

"Thank you for believing me, Chief," Julia said.

"I always believe you, Mrs. Foster."

Julia beamed.

Outside the police station, Holly let out a whoop. "This was the *best* birthday! Newsome, Ventura, and Hammond in one fell swoop. If I had champagne, I'd toast you right here on the sidewalk, Rachel."

"If you had champagne, I'd let you."

"What's she doing here?" Julia asked.

I followed Julia's line of sight. Across the street stood Belinda Almond, shoulders thrown back, a broad smile on her face.

Now I understood. I smiled back and nodded. Belinda was a braver woman than I'd given her credit for, doing what no one else in Juniper Grove had ever done: taken down Jillian Newsome. And for extortion, no less.

Belinda returned my nod and moved on.

"What was that about?" Julia asked.

"Let's find my car," I said. Julia would know in due time, if Belinda wanted her to. It wasn't for me to say.

"It's on the next block up," Holly said.

"Why are you grinning like that?" Julia asked me.

"Because I kind of, sort of solved a case," I replied. "At least I solved parts of it."

"Sure, that's the reason."

Walking down Main Street, I almost skipped like a twelve-year-old. I had to keep pulling myself back, restraining myself, checking my reflection in windows to see if the grin forming on my face was as huge as it felt. To think that hours ago I'd been baffled by a case, bewildered by Belinda, and annoyed by Chief Gilroy. What a difference a few hours could make.

I still thought I wasn't in James Gilroy's ballpark, but I liked him. And liking him, liking the feeling of liking him, was good.

"How about lunch at Wyatt's tomorrow, ladies?" I asked. "It's on me."

FROM THE AUTHOR

We all need a place to escape to from time to time. A place where neighbors drink cups of coffee around a kitchen table (and some indulge in cream puffs), where friends feel safe sharing their hearts' deepest yearnings, where neighbors stop to chat with neighbors outside flower shops. True, the occasional murder mars the Juniper Grove landscape, but what would a mystery series be without dead bodies? Juniper Grove is still that place of escape, and I hope you'll join me there for all the books in the series. I look forward to sharing more of Rachel Stowe and her friends with you.

If you enjoyed *Death of a Dead Man*, please consider leaving a review on Amazon. Nothing fancy, just a couple sentences. Your help is appreciated more than I can say. Reviews make a huge difference in helping readers find the Juniper Grove Mystery Series and in allowing me to continue to write the series. Thank you!

KARIN'S MAILING LIST

For giveaways, exclusive content, and the latest news on the Juniper Grove Mystery Series and future Karin Kaufman books, sign up to the mail and newsletter list at KarinKaufman.com.

MORE BOOKS BY KARIN KAUFMAN

ANNA DENNING MYSTERY SERIES

The Witch Tree
Sparrow House
The Sacrifice
The Club
Bitter Roots
Anna Denning Mystery Series Box Set: Books 1-3

CHILDREN'S BOOKS (FOR CHILDREN AND ADULTS)

The Adventures of Geraldine Woolkins

OTHER BOOKS IN THE JUNIPER GROVE MYSTERY SERIES

Death of a Dead Man
Death of a Scavenger
At Death's Door
Death of a Santa
Scared to Death
Cheating Death
Death Knell